PRAISE FOR SARA MESA

"With short, propulsive chapters, Sara Mesa creates an unforgettable gothic landscape, centered on the mysterious and menacing Wybrany College, that twists in ways that unsettle and thrill. In *Four by Four*, Mesa's sentences are clear as glass, but when you look through you will be terrified by what you see."
—Laura van den Berg, author of *The Third Hotel*

"The atmospheric unraveling of the mystery will keep you turning the page; the ending will leave you stunned—Mesa's *Four by Four* is a tautly written literary thriller that juxtaposes the innocence of children with the fetish of control; a social parable that warns against the silence of oppression and isolation through its disquieting, sparse prose."
—Kelsey Westenberg, Seminary Co-op

"Stylistically, *Four by Four*'s narrative structure is both dazzling and dizzying, as its perfect pacing only enhances the metastasizing dread and dis-ease. . . . Mesa exposes the thin veneer of venerability to be hiding something menacing and unforgivable—and *Four by Four* lays it bare for all the world to see."
—Jeremy Garber, Powell's Books

"Very few authors evoke a visceral reaction with prose in the way that Sara Mesa does. A master of tension building, Mesa constructs lurid phantasmagoric worlds that are equal parts mysterious and unnerving. *Four by Four* sounds an alarm on the dangers of power, privilege, and the self-delusions told in order to hide complicity. A work of high gothic art, *Four by Four* solidifies Mesa as one of the strongest female voices in contemporary Spanish literature."
—Cristina Rodriguez, Deep Vellum Books

"Sara Mesa. Don't forget that name. The finalist for the 30th Premio Herralde de Novela. Read it. Share it. Talk about it. [illegible] You won't be able to put it down."
—Uxue, *Un libro al día*

"Sara Mesa has brought a new [illegible] position to bear important fruit for the [illegible] the twenty first century. . . . *Four by Four* is an [illegible] of the sinister relationships of power corrupted by fear and latent violence that feed this social parable of Kafkian roots."
—Ángel Basanta, *El Mundo*

Four by Four

A NOVEL SARA MESA

Translated by Katie Whittemore

Originally published by Editorial Anagrama S.A. as *Cuatro por cuatro*, 2012

First edition, 2020

Library of Congress Cataloging-in-Publication Data: Available.
ISBN-13: 978-1-948830-14-0 / ISBN-10: 1-948830-14-0

This project and its translation are both supported in part by awards from the National Endowment for the Arts

This project is supported in part by an award from the New York State Council on the Arts with the support of Governor Andrew M. Cuomo and the New York State Legislature

Printed on acid-free paper in the United States of America.

Cover design by Alban Fischer
Interior design by Anthony Blake

Open Letter is the University of Rochester's nonprofit, literary translation press:
Dewey Hall 1-219, Box 278968, Rochester, NY 14627

www.openletterbooks.org

Four by Four

PART ONE

NEVER MORE THAN TWO HUNDRED

CELIA

The contour of the landscape curves, fades, and descends before dissolving in the distance. We are there, at the end, paused and panting under the motionless sky. It's February and still cold. The air cuts off our breath, attacks Teeny's lungs. She's been sick for weeks.

We've never made it this far. Our sneakers are soaked from walking in the muddy grass, avoiding the roads.

We wait for Teeny to catch up and then reconvene.

"Should we have breakfast now?" Valen asks.

Her chubby cheeks tremble. Valen is always hungry. The rest of us protest. It's not time to eat. We only stopped to decide where to go from here, from now. There's no time to waste; we'll eat later, while we walk. Or we won't eat at all.

We have two options: climb the hill until we reach the highway or follow the slope down and try to find the river. Though river is probably an exaggeration. Memory summons to mind a brown thread—a creek, at best—but not its exact location. None of us have been through here in years.

"I say we head for the highway. Then we can hitchhike wherever somebody will take us." Marina sounds braver than she acts. We're not convinced.

I speak up. “Hitchhike? Are you crazy? They’d bring us right back.”

“The river’s safer,” Cristi says.

“But we don’t know where it is!” says Marina.

Cristi shrugs. Valen tries again, reaching for her backpack. “We could eat while we decide.”

“What do you think, Teeny?” I ask.

She looks up. Squints. The lenses of her glasses are fogged over. She coughs again. She coughs and blinks endlessly. Her nose runs. She’s full of fluid, Teeny is. I don’t even wait for her to respond. I speak for her: “Teeny doesn’t care what we do as long as we do it quick. Sitting around in this cold is going to kill her.”

“I think she should eat something,” Valen says.

“Shut up, you greasy fatass,” Cristi says.

They fight. First, with insults. Then they throw themselves on the wet ground and roll around, theatrically, half-heartedly. Marina goads them. It’s not clear whose side she’s on. Teeny and I wait. She thinks about nothing and I try to think about everything.

It doesn’t matter. I see them coming in the 4x4, up the narrow, dusty path. They’re coming toward us and there we are, stopped, as stopped as time. I get a rush: anticipating a lecture from the Booty or punishment from the Headmaster makes me feel better.

A quail chirps in the distance. Valen and Cristi get up, brush off their clothes, and look me in the eye. Neither one speaks, but I know they both blame me.

IGNACIO

Wybrany College, seven o'clock in the evening. Ten, twelve boys in gym clothes hang around to see what's happening. Silence has filled the courtyard at the entrance to the school. Night is falling and Héctor enters escorted by his parents, the Head, and the Advisor. He walks past the boys, glancing up and looking at Ignacio. At him, only him. The look is unmistakable, direct.

Ignacio trembles. The crunch of steps on the gravel lingers. He observes the back of Héctor, his head of full, blond hair, the smooth nape of his neck.

Only when he's roughly shaken does he realize that they've been grumbling in his ear the whole time, and he hasn't heard a thing.

"I'm talking to you, man, can't you hear me?"

Ignacio nods, craning slightly toward the door through which the New Kid has disappeared.

The mother—the woman he assumes is the mother—is outside, closing her umbrella. She has slender calves and iridescent stockings beaded with drizzle. Lux watches her, too, his head cocked and back arched, ready to flee at the slightest movement.

It's November 1st. Ignacio's birthday: twelve years old and finally the prospect of a friend to protect him.

"I said, what do you think of him?" the other boy insists.

"What do I know? I just saw him."

"But he looks queer, right?"

"Yeah. Queer."

Ignacio senses the light is different, more yellow, or hazy. He can't watch Héctor and listen at the same time, but they keep at him and their insistence becomes a command.

"Why queer?" the other boy presses.

"What do you mean, why? You're the one who said it."

"Yeah, but why did you say it, too? What do you know about that?"

A rueful smile breaks on Ignacio's face. Caught again, he thinks, but who cares, he'll finally have a friend to protect him. The New Kid is tall, he's strong, and out of all the faces there in the courtyard, he chose to look at Ignacio's.

He hears the girls' laughter from the other side of the wall, a restless laughter, musical. He longs for girls, but only as classmates.

"Because he laughs like a girl."

"Oh, so you've heard him laugh?"

"Yeah, before. When he got here."

"Really? Where?"

He frees himself from the arm that grabs him.

"I don't know, before. Let go of me, I have to get to class."

"Class? Classes are over."

"Just let me go," he begs.

"Cripple, sissy, fucking fag," the other boy says, releasing him.

Ignacio hobbles away in his raised shoe with the lift. Laughter screeches at his back.

Real or imagined, Ignacio hears it all the time.

HÉCTOR'S ORIGINS

But the New Kid's origins go back to some time before, to weeks before, days before; not that time matters much in this place, where the days are so like one another. They accumulate, piling up, creating a sense of continuity, movement, or the evolution of something.

It's important to note, perhaps, that Héctor isn't present on this occasion. Just his mother, or the woman who looks like the mother, and the father—him, for sure—in the Headmaster's office. They are joined by the assistant headmistress of school, alias "the Booty."

The office doesn't seem like an office. It's more like a magnificent living room, with its crystal chandeliers and perfectly-worn Persian rugs—vulgar, if they're too new—and gleaming floor-to-ceiling windows, the glass spotless and free of flies.

Seated in leather armchairs around a low table, they speak for a long time with the particular stiffness to which they are accustomed.

The Booty—a real beauty, in another time—discreetly keeps her distance. Only when necessary does she add an opportune fact, blinking before she speaks. In general, such facts relate to fees, services, and requirements, details of which the Headmaster is ignorant, given that he delegates this minutia to her.

The tone of the conversation is sickly-sweet, good manners, slightly soured.

The office smells like cologne. Which one? Impossible to say. A mix of various scents: those worn by the people now present, and by those who are absent. The people who sat where they are now, finalizing the details of their progeny's matriculation.

The scent of the elite, one could say if it weren't an oversimplification, since that isn't exactly the case. But one couldn't claim the opposite is true, either.

"You do realize we're making an exception . . ."

"We know, we know," Héctor's father says.

He moves his hands to accentuate his words, like he did when he was a government minister. Unnecessary rhetorical emphasis.

"It will be more expensive—due to the exception, you understand—still, you insist this is what you want?"

"Yes, we insist. It's absolutely critical."

"Though it won't be easy for us, getting rid of the boy," the woman adds.

"*Getting rid of* isn't quite the right expression," the father says. His eyes flash. He looks at his wife and she goes quiet.

The Booty smiles at them both. They shouldn't feel uncomfortable, she says, language betrays us all. Parents undeniably feel a sense of relief when they enroll their children at the college; it happens to everyone. Bringing up a child is complicated, an act of responsibility demanding extreme dedication. There's nothing wrong with leaving a piece of it in the hands of experts.

"Héctor is a brilliant boy," the woman continues, speaking cautiously now. "Very intelligent, headstrong, a bit mischievous, maybe. He always finds a way to make his uniform unique somehow: a patch, a hole, a button pinned somewhere. As you know, he needs to do things his way."

"Ah, but that's good," the Headmaster says. "That's very good. It speaks of character, strength of character, manliness. We don't go overboard on rules here. Strict on the fundamentals, flexible on incidentals. Our educational methods are liberal, they're based in absolute freedom. Will you have some . . ." He turns to look at Lux, the cat, who has just slipped through the bars on the window, ". . . coffee?"

They drink from little porcelain cups, served with biscuits they barely nibble. Then they settle the rest: the registration, monthly payments, additional installments. The visitors express their surprise that rooms are shared, but nod sensibly at the explanation.

"At this age, boys on their own are hard to control," says the Booty. "This way they keep an eye on each other. It's not to their benefit to be alone in their free time."

"Obviously, some boarding schools make private rooms a mainstay of their appeal," the Headmaster continues, "precisely because they have nothing else to offer. Special menus, the latest technology, professional sports facilities, blah, blah, blah . . . They're only focused on the superfluous aspects. We guarantee a sufficient level of material comfort. Not excellent, perhaps, but sufficient. But we also guarantee an extraordinarily high-quality education, which goes far beyond academics. We do not impose discipline: the children impose it on themselves. Rigorous, not rigid. Firm, not harsh. Personalities are sculpted, polished until they shine. The country's best have passed through here. We know how to shape the best."

He carefully cleans his beard with a napkin and waits for a reaction. The couple smiles. They are notably, visibly relaxed.

An agreement has been reached.

THE FOUNDER

Wybrany College—which we pronounce *güíbrani colich*—is set in a man-made meadow surrounded by forested terrain.

On the highway from Cárdenas to the now defunct city of Vado, no sign exists indicating access to the property. Supposedly, this is in order to avoid any invasion of privacy by those who would pry, including journalists.

The Wybrany College website neither provides an exact location, nor are there any photographs of its facilities. Only a brief contact form available for interested parents that, once submitted, apparently never receives a response.

In any case, full occupancy at Wybrany College is not a concern. There is likely a long waitlist for any openings: this is one of the best schools in the country. Héctor is the only student we've seen arrive recently, except for the first years and the Specials. Adding a cohort of Specials was a later expansion of the school. In no way did this alter the spirit of the college's founding.

The history of Wybrany College is recited once a year. The assistant headmistress describes it during the mid-January anniversary celebration, in a formal speech prior to the dance.

The way she tells it, the school was founded in 1943 by a Polish businessman forced into exile during the Second World War. He arrived in our country practically ruined, despite having been one of the wealthiest men in Europe just two years before.

The assistant headmistress reads her speech before the silent auditorium: "*Moved by the fate of exiled orphans who had lost their parents, Andrzej Wybrany directed his efforts at building a school where they could be educated and cared for with all the resources they would have enjoyed had the destinies of their families remained unaltered.*"

In this version, Wybrany College was an elite alternative to the orphanages and shelters of the day.

Naturally, Wybrany College was not founded in 1943. The school is quite a bit newer than that. It is rumored to be no more than fifteen years old. The same time frame, more or less, as the depopulation of Vado.

The fact that it was built in the style of the 1940s—solemn buildings arranged in the shape of a 'C,' high stone walls, orderly grounds, shady bowers—doesn't actually mean anything, as one can easily imagine.

Following the trail like bloodhounds, we can see that those elements of design have been incorporated into the modern necessities as well: the golf course, the helipad, the tennis courts, the four swimming pools.

A hidden outline betrays the present in the past, tracing the lines drawn by fear.

THE EXAMINATION

The Headmaster takes the floor, and his first line of questioning is predictable.

"Where were you girls planning to go?" His voice creaks. He clears his throat and repeats the question.

"Where were you girls planning to go?"

I smile and don't answer. The Booty speaks next. Nothing new. "Where were you girls planning to go?"

I watch her become desperate. I tell them I can't answer a question directed at "you girls," in the plural. I can say where *I* planned to go, but I can't speak for the others. In fact, I don't understand why they have called me in but not them.

"Because you were the one who organized it. On that point they all agree," the Booty says.

"They don't agree on the other points?"

"We're asking the questions, not you."

Time and again they ask me the same thing: where were we planning to go. They know as well as I do, so I don't see any reason to repeat it. I prefer to tell them what we were *not* planning to do.

"It wasn't an escape. We were going to come back."

The Booty resumes the interrogation. She is obviously at ease in these situations.

"Come back? Come back when? You wanted to make it to Cárdenas. You can't walk there and back in one day."

"If you know that's where we were going, why do you keep asking me?"

"Because I don't know whether or not Cárdenas was just one stop on a longer trip."

"I already told you it wasn't."

The Advisor hesitates, lifts his hand, requests to speak. Short, hairy, with a bulbous nose and wide hips, he has an unhealthy look that does not inspire respect.

"I think we ought to put ourselves in the girl's position," he says.

The *girl*, the *boys*, the *children*: this is the way that counselors express themselves. The Booty turns to him with contempt; the Headmaster laughs quietly to himself, the left corner of his lip slightly curled.

"Under different circumstances, her parents would be here to defend her, or at least support her," he continues. "But this girl has no one."

"Exactly," says the Booty. "Exactly. She has no one, yet she has been given this opportunity. She could be living in the outskirts of Cárdenas, but here she is, enjoying the college's facilities. She has no appreciation for how lucky she is. Moreover, she riles up the other girls. I don't understand why we should put ourselves in her position."

They argue. It's easy to tune them out. It's all too predictable. I prefer to watch the Booty and the Advisor exchange arguments and rebuttals, the power struggle that tips the scales back and forth, never committing entirely to either side. I can see that the Headmaster feels the same way. He almost looks amused, turning his head from one to the other as they serve and return. Clearly, our attempted escape does not concern him in the least; this time around, he's not even curious. I watch him out of the corner of my eye. He pretends not to notice.

They agree to subject me to closer monitoring, not in order to control me, but for my own good. Only and exclusively for my own good, the Booty says. When she says it, she fixes me with a watery stare. The Advisor commits fully to the plan.

Close monitoring is one of his specialties, it seems.

I see that they don't consider this surveillance a punishment.

It is what it is, there's nothing I can do.

I consent.

THE FIRST DAY

The New Kid is there, at the start of the day. He's not "Héctor" yet, but will be soon. He sits in the back row and speaks to no one.

And there, at the front of the room, Ignacio's defenseless neck.

He can feel the New Kid's gaze. It makes him happy and he yearns for the pricking it provokes.

The others horse around, trying to get the New Kid's attention. He looks like a leader and they have to earn it.

Instead, he stares through a filter of hazy morning light. A melancholy light that conceals both the athletic fields and his hard, metallic eyes.

It's the first cool morning after a relentless summer that stretched on interminably. Today, all the students are wearing long sleeves except for him. He crosses his muscular arms on the desk and presses his lips tightly together, his face turned.

He barely opens his mouth the whole morning, not even to answer the teachers' questions. He insists on an obstinate and continual *I don't know, I don't remember, no.* Stubborn, difficult. A fist. His nails, turned white from holding his tongue. What's he got inside? Ignacio wonders. Why did he look at me yesterday, only at me, why did he turn around and choose me, and why is he still staring, staring so hard?

He attempts to establish telepathic communication—to no avail.

Ignacio believes in telepathy. He believes it is a purer form of communication than verbal language. The words that reach us are tainted; there is interference, always. Two minds that speak honestly, cleanly, across broad and efficient channels, free of weeds, like a highway: this is his ideal language.

Meanwhile, the whispers under the tables start to lose their strength. *Queer, fucking fag.* They travel from desk to desk, but more tenuously, without conviction.

Ignacio floats above his seat, his neck hot from being watched.

TEENY

Although her mother is just a handsbreadth taller, Teeny is small in other ways. Faced with Teeny's ungainliness, the mother is elegant indeed. Elegantly, she demonstrates her joy at seeing her daughter, pulls her close and looks to see who is watching. Her pupils dilate, more unease than excitement in the trembling of her hands.

Teeny hardly notices. She prances nervously, coughs a little. Her nose leaks.

"Poor thing, you're sick, darling."

A stammer. Better, I'm better, Teeny whispers.

She unwraps the gifts. Sneakers with laces, a planner, books of stories, many stories—reading is good, reading is *so* healthy, the mother thinks that only readers will save themselves in this dark world. Fairies, white rabbits, pastel colors on the cover. Teeny is no longer a little girl. She bites her lip as she flips through the pages, but doesn't complain. She only asks: Papá?

He couldn't come, the mother says, fluffing her hair. He'll be back from Germany on Sunday, and she can see him then, before returning to the *colich*. An extra weekend, she exclaims, glancing around, you didn't expect that, did you, darling!

It's because Teeny is sick. One weekend away a month, that's the norm, that's what everyone knows and accepts without issue.

But her nose is always running and she coughs all the time. She's smaller than the other girls, skinny and pale, she squints and has something of an overbite; perhaps therein lies the exception.

She has Turner syndrome, but she's intelligent, her mother said the day of her official enrollment.

Now she repeats it every chance she gets. Turner syndrome. It has an artistic ring to it: bridges in the mist, families struggling against misfortune's blows. She can attend the *colich* because she's intelligent, the mother claims at every turn. She took charge of fighting like a lioness for permission to matriculate Teeny. She even appeared in a magazine article, a new Mother Courage, triumphant, smiling, dressed in designer labels.

"The cold this February has been bad for her. And she partook in a certain field trip, one not organized by *us*, I'm afraid. I'm sure she'll tell you all about it, right?" The Booty stared hard at Teeny as she said this.

Field trip? Her soaking wet feet, the frightening pre-breakfast walk. Where were you going, darling? the mother will ask later, when they leave the office. Oh, Celia, the famous Celia, always getting other girls in trouble, she should have stayed in Cárdenas with her biological mother—she spits out the syllables *bi-o-log-i-cal*—some people will simply never appreciate their opportunities.

Ungrateful people, you see, ungrateful.

They walk, holding hands, their bodies silhouetted in the light of Friday afternoon. Teeny stumbles, like always, on her thin little sparrow's ankles. The mother's extra height dips low, too, in haste, determination, and disgust.

THE ADVISOR

They call me in for a little chat, and I prepare myself for another round of questioning. But we don't go to the Booty's office. The door opens and the person standing there is a man, not a woman.

A smile hangs off his lips as he comes to take my hands in his. I stammer, I don't manage a word, but I allow him to guide me to a sofa, where I sit.

He brings me lemonade.

"Oh Celia, Celia, you suffer so . . ."

I'm still wary. He doesn't reproach me. He seems to understand. This is unnerving.

He knows I'm not like the others. He says so.

"You aren't like the others."

And then he adds, solemnly: "But you could be."

I tell him that's not what I want. What I want is to go back to where I come from.

He smiles gently and asks if I would like to have a pet. A cat, perhaps.

I'm not surprised. He pretends to be simple in order to win me over, that's all. But a cat is tempting. He's done his research and knows that I like them. That I miss my old Tinaja. I'm tempted.

"They'd let me?"

"Of course they'd let you. I'll take care of it. To each according to his needs. We've always said so."

"All right. But I need to go."

He kneels at my side. His breath closes in on me. Sweet, heavy. I try to concentrate on my future cat. I like them too much not to be pleased.

I can barely hear him whisper. *Venga,* come on, come on, he murmurs, but I don't know what he's referring to.

Venga, venga, venga, he repeats.

I think he's trying to comfort me, but I'm not sure. I stand up. He continues to kneel, absurdly, and speaks from down on the floor.

"I understand you, Celia. I understand your confusion. But nothing will happen to you if you trust me. I'll look out for you."

I don't answer. I don't have anything to say.

He continues. "You mustn't stir up the others. Especially Teeny. The girls on scholarship can handle themselves, they're made of the same stuff you are. But Teeny is different. She's too weak. You already know that she's sick."

He's right about that. I don't want to lose Teeny. But, an unhealthy thought crosses my mind: if I had a cat, then I wouldn't need her anymore. Is Teeny my pet? Is that what I want her for?

I pick up the paperweight from his desk. A small crystal ball with a picture of a bird on its base. The bird is wearing a king's crown. A ridiculous image.

He finally stands, comes toward me. I put the paperweight back in its place. He picks it up and moves closer, ball in hand.

"Do you want it?"

I say no. He opens my fist, places the paperweight on my palm, closes my fingers one by one, slowly. I let him.

"I'm going to take you to see your mother," he says. "I promise."

Pricking of the eyes. Tingling. I'm not sure of the source of the tingling, or his offer.

My mother.

"But you're not going to like what you see. Be warned. Things have changed a lot in a short time."

"Will it be a secret?" I ask.

"Oh yes, of course. You mustn't tell anyone."

THE ROOM

Telepathy is useless to him. Héctor is assigned to another room, exactly three doors down. He would need to be closer to prevent the punches, the insults.

These first days of class, Héctor has watched him constantly. He pays close attention to Ignacio, compared to the indifference he shows everyone else. Ignacio feels singled out and this comforts him and makes him brave.

He sits on his bunk and scratches hard between his toes. He dares to speak.

"All the rooms are full. Why'd they assign him that one?"

Iván comes over.

"Because he has to sleep somewhere, idiot. I saw them bring a cot. I have no idea what his parents would say if they found out. Paying a ton of money for a crappy fold-up bed."

Carlos, from the depths of the bottom bunk.

"Oh, they'll find out. What's weird is that they even let him in. He was held back. The *colich* doesn't take those kids. Especially once school's already started."

Iván muses.

"Maybe it's because that girl left. You heard they expelled a Special this year, right?"

And he adds: "But if you think about it, if they were down a girl, another one should have come. We're not even now. When we leave, one of us will be on our own."

Carlos closes the conversation.

"Specials don't count, anyway. They're worthless."

They're worthless, yes. On this the boys agree. And they agree not to call Héctor queer anymore. They don't feign disinterest now. They listen for noises in the hallway, hoping to distinguish his voice from the others. Cruelty has given way to surveillance.

"Doesn't he ever talk? The bastard," Iván says.

"Maybe he's shy," Ignacio summons the strength to suggest.

Loud laughter from Carlos unnerves him.

"The New Kid's high all day, that's what's up. Come on, he's totally got weed. And I'm gonna ask him as soon as he trusts me. He's not fucking shy."

"Man, if he gets you weed, score some for the rest of us," Iván laughs.

Ignacio laughs, too. His own laughter sounds almost strange. Surprisingly, they leave him alone that night. He lies back in bed, hugging his pillow. The little light from the switch glows green on his cheek.

He listens, strains to hear something. Nothing but the *tap-tap-tap* of water dripping in the sink and the whine of the mastiff Cayetana, Lux's pitiful meows.

But not Héctor's voice, which he would recognize no matter what.

He begins to speak to him telepathically, insistently. His lips move soundlessly, so he won't get teased, or hit.

By the time he's overcome by sleep, he still hasn't received an answer.

VALEN, CRISTI & MARINA

Teeny is back with a little color in her cheeks, her hair smoothed with a straightening iron.

She's blanketed in compliments—Valen, Cristi, and Marina lay it on thick. What did she bring them? She knows that's their motivation: Teeny is generous with the Specials. They wait for her precisely because she's generous.

They go to the girls' bathroom to avoid raising suspicions among the Normals.

Teeny doles out her attention as she doles out the gifts.

Valen chews candy and sucks her spit.

Cristi, exasperated: "Ugh, do you have to be so tacky?"

Celia isn't with them. When it gets dark, she goes running in the Adidas sneakers donated by Wybrany. Her shadow can be seen in the distance, a gust trampling the wet grass. Back and forth in a mostly errant, undisciplined race.

They watch her from inside the doorway, and from their little huddle rise murmurs and complaints.

Teeny demurs, but weakly. "Celia didn't say anything about us." Her nose drips. "She took all the blame."

"Well, then she's saying that she manipulated us," Cristi says. "And I think that's true. She never stopped to think about the consequences of her big idea. Such bullshit. We almost got seriously punished, you know. She's selfish. Come on, Teeny—why do you think she hangs out with you? You're not part of our group. She's totally taking advantage of you."

Teeny tilts her head. She doesn't know whether to deny it or nod in agreement. Instinctually, feebly, she whispers: "My house is in Cárdenas, too. Maybe that's why."

How could that possibly be the reason, the others say. Julia's parents also live in Cárdenas. Her mother was mayor and now she has some other big position. And Teeny's house, she has to admit, is in the city center, next to the National Museum. Not in Celia's neighborhood, on the outskirts. Every city is made up of different cities, Cristi says. Even she's surprised by how intelligent she sounds and smiles to herself.

What's most perplexing about Celia isn't that she's from Cárdenas, but the question of how she came to be at the *colich* at all. Who recommended her for a scholarship, who granted it, why just for her senior year? Nobody knows. Rumors point to a friend of her mother's, someone with connections, perhaps. But this *colich* thing is too much for Celia, they say. She had gotten used to the robberies, the looting, an easy life free of rules. Now she's here, a caged animal.

The girls talk like ventriloquists and Teeny timidly agrees. She folds herself into a corner, skinny little arms hugging her body, and coughs like an old toy poodle.

Marina brushes her hair furiously. Static lifts her bangs, which wave above her small, close-set eyes.

"Well, she can count me out for sure. They really came down on us, thanks to her."

"And it's not like she can do anything on her own," Cristi says.

"She uses us because she can't do it by herself," says Valen, not entirely convinced.

Teeny—her voice ground down by the others—repeats herself again and again until they hear her. "She didn't force us to go with her. We all wanted to. It sounded fun."

"She should just go back to her neighborhood," Marina says. "I'm sure she misses it."

"What's her neighborhood like?" Cristi asks.

"Rats, hooligans, graffiti, needles, all of that." Marina wrinkles her nose.

"And people like that?"

"Of course. People who grow up there *want* that. They complain if you take them out. Like Celia."

They hear her coming down the hallway, her ragged breath reaching them.

They cover up by pretending to show each other their tits, as they've done on other occasions.

They discuss how they've grown, their shape, color, variation in the nipples. Then they agree on a vote-based, numerical ranking.

When it's her turn, Teeny lifts her shirt and bares two pale, tiny little sacks at her ribs. The girls laugh at the hint of breasts that aren't really anything at all. Celia joins the group and sees Teeny; she laughs, too, pointing out the bit of fuzz that grows on her nipples.

Teeny blushes and covers herself quickly. She looks away, unsure which expression will best hide her discomfort.

THE BOOTY

The Booty pays the occasional visit to the Headmaster's office. Sometimes she notifies him beforehand, but often she goes without any warning.

Her coloring is different after those meetings. Fine, zigzagging veins lace the apples of her cheeks. Her eyes tend to shine, oily, and she walks—staggers—like a drunk woman.

What happens in that office concerns no one but the two of them, yet it swells through the school day like an underground tide, its fluctuations leaving an inexorable mark. The whole *colich*—teachers and students alike—feels the flow of that more or less secret relationship.

Inside that room, the Booty humiliates herself while the Headmaster sits impassively or snorts cocaine. Sprawled comfortably in his chair, arms crossed over his chest, he watches and speaks to her slowly. His sentences are short, lacerating, and he doesn't squander them.

"It's sad to look at you. Not just pathetic—useless. You're rotten, you know that? You're spoiled. There's nothing in your veins but pus, or poison."

He enjoys the show, her obstinate silence, for a short time—five minutes, half an hour—or the whole afternoon. She's in no hurry. He directs her what to do, how to position herself. She obeys. She submits without complaint. She'll only spit her reproaches later, as she dresses, never even having been touched.

"No one knows what a fake you are."

The Headmaster laughs, and sometimes responds.

"Of course they do. You know it, and you still come. The children's parents know it, and they still send them. Those same children know it, and still they admire me."

"They don't admire you, they fear you."

"No, darling. They fear *you*. Do you know what you represent for them? A weed."

"A weed?"

"Yes, a dried up weed." He laughs.

"You could have had me long before we came to this."

"I could have, but I didn't want you. It excited me more to have you at a distance, when you were appealing. Now I enjoy myself a different way. It's a question of nuance."

The Booty slows her movements, takes her time rolling up her pantyhose so he'll continue to insult her.

But he doesn't. He metes them out in doses. He watches her dress, scowling in disgust. The lamp casts a greenish-yellow light. The Headmaster likes her—prefers her—like this.

The Booty also seeks that light, and craves it when she's denied.

THE NIGHT

They're not allowed to leave their rooms and there are always snitches prepared to rat them out. But Ignacio sneaks out anyway, tripping over his pajama bottoms. Shadows overlap in the hallway. He feels his way along the wall.

On other nights he's heard the scuff of footsteps, footsteps that didn't exist before the New Kid came. The New Kid, who after a week of classes, is just Héctor, now. And as he earned his name, he broke his stubborn silence with monosyllables and the odd, short sentence. To Ignacio, everything Héctor says is an expression of his audacity.

He admires him blindly.

Ignacio goes in search of those footsteps, a moment to speak with him alone.

He advances slowly—alert and hopeful—and his eyes adjust to the dark.

He makes out Héctor's door and stands outside, sifting through the sounds of the sleeping boys. He concentrates on the silence and tries to sense his hero's presence. He waits and hears no more than the murmur of a dream—a nightmare, maybe—and Ignacio, defeated, turns back toward his room. But then, heavy breath at his back.

His heart leaps before he can turn.

He spins around as the hand grips his shoulder like a claw, squeezing his bones.

The face isn't Héctor's. Almond eyes, wide jaw, and greater stature reveal Adrián, alias the Goon.

The Goon squeezes him harder and punches him in the stomach. What the hell is he doing there? Spying on them? Is he one of the Booty's rats?

His punches don't make a sound, but they hurt. Ignacio falls to the ground and protects himself with his arms and knees.

"Leave me alone!" he shouts. "I couldn't sleep! I was just taking a walk. I wasn't spying on anyone!"

The Goon looks down at him, his face distorted by the angle. Sleepy voices of curious boys hungry for a fight, stirring behind the doors.

No matter how he aches for Héctor, none of the voices are his.

The cat arrives and it's a small Persian with a wrinkled face and just the hint of a nose, wet and squished like rat shit. I would've preferred a Roman cat, one off the street.

"But a stray is always more trouble," the Advisor tells me. "It would run for the woods and you'd lose it right away. This is a unique specimen, genetically altered to be gentler, smaller. Look, it barely even has claws. It's designed to be with people. A stray cat is a selfish animal: it uses you. It doesn't want your company. You wouldn't like that, would you?"

"It must have cost a lot of money," I say.

The Advisor dribbles around this. He's skilled at keeping possession of the conversation.

"Don't worry about the money. Money is no object as long as it makes you happy. Wybrany doesn't waste—we invest."

I hold the animal under its belly. The kitten meows, indifferent, and moves its small, hairy paws. I don't want it. I say it with my face, without a word.

"Celia, dear, it's the thought that counts. When someone does something for you, out of kindness, you musn't reject it."

"It isn't moral to spend that kind of money on this when there are plenty of stray cats," I insist.

"It's not immoral. What do you know about what is or isn't moral? You're still too young to be talking about those things."

The Advisor doesn't reprimand me. His tone is sweet, deliberate. I can't argue with him, nor do I want to. I put the cat down and look at it in disgust.

"You promised you'd take me to Cárdenas."

The Advisor nods. A new expression forms on his face—a tautness in the arch of his brow—and then he speaks: "I promised you and I'll follow through. I only ask for a little patience. We have to find the right time. And remember: not a word to anyone."

"Are you asking me to lie?"

His eyes harden. He turns toward the window, as if looking for courage. The right thing to say. I watch as he considers my question. His face is bathed in shadow. I attack again: "You always say that lying is the greatest betrayal we can commit against ourselves."

He traps my pass, thinks a moment, and shoots: "But Plato spoke of the 'noble lie' and believed there were lies similar to truths."

I don't remember hearing this in Philosophy class, and I say so.

"There are many things you haven't heard yet," he responds. "There are many things you still have to learn."

He picks up the cat and shows it to me again, smiling.

"I'll take care of it myself, don't you worry. At least until you change your mind. One cannot avoid one's responsibility—we can't return it simply because you don't want it. Now, that would be immoral."

I get up. I'm getting tired of his speech. He lets me go.

But before I reach the door, he raises a hand to stop me.

"I'll call him Lux. But we can change the name if you don't like it. Remember: you will always have the final say over this animal. I will act only as an intermediary."

THE TEACHER

There is a new teacher. Young. Héctor looks at her differently.

She looks back at him from behind her reading glasses. Her eyes are icy and move constantly.

She waves her hands as she talks about social movements, revolutions, monarchies, republics that follow one after another, about dictatorships and democracies, calling on students randomly, spontaneously, and surely, a flurry that always ends with Héctor, in the back row. She rests a finger lightly on her desk and makes him repeat what she's just said.

He repeats, parsimoniously, each of her words one by one. The only difference is his maturing voice, the boy he was and is no longer occasionally surfacing.

"I always listen to you," he says one morning. "You don't have to test me."

She inspects him in silence.

The class is quiet.

Ignacio turns his head very slowly and sees them staring at each other, and the way they look at each other stabs him in the stomach.

"How old are you?" she asks.

"Thirteen."

"And why are you here, if you're thirteen?"

Surely she knows. She's only asking to humiliate him.

"I stayed back a year, in another school."

"What kind of school? One like this? Or public?"

"No, not public. Not like this, either."

The other students hold their breath, watching them. The air thickens when they look at each other. At times, she seems impatient, annoyed, but never flustered.

The new teacher is a rival, distracting Héctor, drawing him away from Ignacio.

Ignacio bows his head over his desk and purrs like Lux. The telepathic connections aren't always present, and when they are, the messages arrive clouded with interference.

Language is useless. Words are corrupt and he doesn't know how to go back to the beginning.

THE WIFE

The Headmaster has a wife, and she comes to the *colich* to see him every once in a while, at irregular intervals.

The Booty never knows ahead of time when she will have to suspend her office visits. Only when she sees the wife's car—a pigeon-shit-resistant minivan—parked next to his does the Booty retreat, resigned and in pain.

The Headmaster's house enjoys views of Wybrany's facilities: the immense grassy park and paths of packed earth, the stain of the forest crowding the metal fence stitched with CCTV cameras. The house is solid and luxurious with large windows, classically decorated but with all the comforts of home automation.

To the left, the Booty's home is plainer, more feminine perhaps. She adorns it with dried flowers, porcelain, a shrine of framed pictures setting off her face, beautiful in earlier years.

The Advisor just has a room, en suite, like the other teachers at the *colich*. This seems to satisfy him. He claims not to be attached to material things. It's rumored he has—or had—a thin, bony girlfriend whose picture presides over his desk. It must be a sporadic relationship, because no one has ever seen her visit, and he himself (he claims) rarely leaves the *colich*.

So it's just the Headmaster who has a spouse, a smooth-looking spouse: silky hair and silky clothes, a quality to her flesh that the Booty now lacks.

She comes occasionally, and when she comes she shuts herself in the house with the Headmaster and no sounds come from inside—no voices or laughter, moans or shouts.

The Booty leans on her windowsill and incessantly watches the Headmaster's house. She performs mental exercises, trying to picture herself from the outside. She always imagines herself differently: not idealized, but different, yes.

Though she misses him, she's accustomed to his absence: the Headmaster is known to spend long periods of time away from the *colich*. Even she doesn't know where he is sometimes, or how long he'll be away. When he could reappear. He simply takes his car and leaves. Other times, he uses a chauffeur or is collected by private helicopter.

He'll appear unexpectedly, randomly. Then he'll set off to tour the classrooms, surprise inspections accompanied by the Booty, who is swollen and satisfied by his return. He smiles with an impeccable set of teeth and hitches his pants above his waist, pretentious, as she questions the teachers. She doesn't stop to hear their answers. They stroll between the desks and their eyes slide over notebooks, computers, over the bent heads of the students.

And with every pass, it's like they've turned the page of a book.

BEATINGS

The days are slow and marked by a steely cold, the railing that runs down to the fields increasingly frozen and damp.

Despite the beatings, Ignacio still waits for a connection.

They hit him routinely, rhythmically, taking turns, every day, every evening. They spit in his face, steal his food, his school supplies, money. They take his sheets and blankets and he spends the night curled up, trembling on the bare mattress.

He doesn't ever rebel, doesn't tell anyone what's happening. He understands this is the price he must pay for living alongside his classmates. It doesn't even seem wrong. He doesn't think about things in those terms.

Sometimes there are marks—everyone sees them when he changes for gym—but no one ever says anything. No one thinks it's strange, in any case.

When a bruise turns yellow, another one—violet—appears. There are always stains of various colors on Ignacio's legs, his arms, sometimes on his bony, boyish face. They even split his lip, a fact that bothers no one.

But last week, the Advisor takes him out of the line at practice, leads him over to a corner and touches the bruise on his thigh.

"What's going on here?" he asks.

Ignacio sputters an unsatisfactory answer. When he sets himself to it, the Advisor knows how to interrogate. But Ignacio remains impassive, even feels proud of his silence, despite his questioner's tactics.

The Advisor is pensive for a moment, then states:

"If you don't report them, you're complicit as well."

Complicit, sure, but Ignacio expects the beatings, he's grown up with them. He thinks, perhaps, that his telepathic efforts will lead directly to Héctor, his savior.

He believes in his religion. He subscribes fully to its asceticism and penitence.

THE WOODS

I follow the fence, watching the woods. I know how to get out. I know where the holes are. Everyone knows about them, I think, but they all keep quiet.

In any case, the woods are forbidden. Supposedly, they're dangerous. Not because of animals or the rough terrain, but the possibility of vagabonds, thieves, terrorists: people who want to blow up what this world is becoming.

There were field trips in the past. Field trips to collect plants for botany class, dirt and water samples for experiments on oxidation and weather.

But now the woods are contaminated—a toxic spill in the river—so they're not even good for that.

The gaps in the fence put the *colich* in jeopardy: an outside that could enter, catching us off-guard in the middle of the night.

But I come from outside and I'm not afraid.

For me, this comfort is exile.

I think about the Advisor, about how I can manipulate him, and it's then that the owl flies over my head, its call suspended in the sky. A long, reedy cry that flaps clumsily toward me.

Hoo-hoo-hoo-hoo-hoo.

The mastiff Cayetana lifts her muzzle and sniffs at the owl's trail as it flies away. She's also unsettled. The sun is setting and the light retreats brusquely, violently.

The night speaks and you just have to listen carefully to hear it.

I pace the fence once more, dragging my feet. I don't feel like running today.

Covered in shadow, the school's buildings are sketches in the distance. Our brightly painted building is shorter, more modern; experimental architecture for an experiment we participate in unknowingly.

The lights are shining in the dorms and I can imagine how warm and comfortable they are inside.

The nicer it is in there, the more disturbing it is to go out.

My classmates used to come with me. We held each other's arms and advanced as a united front, protection against the suspicions of the Normal girls, and the boys who were mouthier with us than with them.

Now they stay inside and seem more and more like the others.

Even Valen wants to lose weight now, though she still eats around the clock. She craves the slender figures of the other girls. Julia's. Teeny's mother's.

The screech owl marks its territory with its cry. A warning for me: get out, these woods are mine.

The owl doesn't want any competition. Neither do I.

GERASIM

Since Ignacio's conversation with the Advisor, things have slowly started to change for him. It's possible that the Advisor alerted the Headmaster to his circumstances, and that's why he's become interested in Ignacio and fixes him with his usual, steady stare.

Something about the boy is seductive. The Headmaster is drawn to his submission, that passive acceptance of his fate. A sweetness that has yet to be—is about to be—corrupted. This excites him irrepressibly.

Ignacio is poised to transform. In that fateful moment of adolescence when everything could change with a single word or gesture. Each day might be critical.

The Headmaster wants to be part of that process.

When the boy is at his side, he's overcome with a strange feeling of contentment. He makes a habit of bringing him to his office now and then.

"Oh Gerasim, my Gerasim," he greets him.

The Headmaster reclines in his armchair, asks him to read from a newspaper or book. He closes his eyes as Ignacio recites. Sometimes he dozes off, even snores once in a while. Sometimes, as compensation, the Headmaster gives him gifts. Small, valuable objects that don't make the other children jealous, but which they will steal, nonetheless: a feather, a magnifying glass, small wooden carvings, trading cards, a compass, gifts from another time that return the Headmaster to his own childhood.

He calls him Gerasim. Ignacio doesn't know why, but neither does he dare to ask. He doesn't understand any of what's going on; he listens to the Headmaster speak, his brief, metaphysical digressions about the world. Ignacio thinks maybe this is all okay, he folds himself up at the Headmaster's feet like a little dog and lets him gently stroke his head. He isn't the protector Ignacio was seeking, but he resigns himself to the idea.

One day, the Headmaster tries to explain.

"There's a book, a very famous Russian book, that tells the story of a rich man who becomes ill and is about to die. This man had everything in life: money, power, fame, a lovely family, splendid home. But in his illness, he begins to feel very alone. He becomes aware that his life has been nothing more than decoration, a meaningless pastiche. Now that he's sick, no one can stand to see him twisting in pain; nobody wants to hear his complaints or cries. Not his family, not even his best friends. It's a terrible story," he concludes. "A man is dying and is alone."

He pauses. Ignacio hangs on his words but doesn't understand. They sit in silence for several minutes. Only the ticking of the wall clock is heard, the distant voices of the boys playing paddleball. The Headmaster continues, smiling weakly now.

"The man can only be soothed by resting his feet on the shoulders of a young, healthy servant, the only one who doesn't feign compassion, but truly feels it."

He stops speaking and observes Ignacio closely.

"And then what happens?"

"What happens? It doesn't matter what happens. His servant provides relief. The man doesn't want to see anyone else, not even his children. That's what happens."

"But does he die?"

"Of course he dies."

Ignacio feels slightly disappointed. The story sounds too simple to be in such a famous book. A sick man. A man in terrible pain who only feels better when he puts his feet on the shoulders of his servant. A rich man dies. That's all.

Why has the Headmaster told him this story? He thinks that maybe he's trying to establish a comparison, but he's not a servant, he isn't strong, he doesn't feel compassion—real or fake—for the Headmaster, who—it goes without saying—has never put his feet on Ignacio's shoulders. He stammers:

"Are you sick, sir?"

The Headmaster stares at him. His eyes shine, deep in their purple, flabby sockets. He nods softly, slowly.

"Yes, my dear Gerasim. I am very sick."

He's wearing different clothes—the formal uniform with large commemorative pins, and instead of a polo, the white shirt with starched cuffs—but the same whispers follow him. Muffled laughter, insults, pinches that hurt more than punches.

Marina's father has polished the floor. Ignacio sees himself reflected in the tiles, his faceless silhouette more attractive, less damning somehow.

Héctor's height rises before him, a few meters ahead. He laughs casually with the others and no longer looks at Ignacio at all.

Ignacio passes the table of scholarship students, a reflection of Wybrany's circular justice, and notices the empty chair. Just nineteen of the seats are taken, nineteen Specials. The empty chair fills his eyes, distracting him.

Where could she be, the girl they expelled? He only vaguely remembers her, an older girl, dark, intense, the memory so blurry he can't even make something up about her absence.

There's no more time for distractions. The Goon pinches him again, twisting his arm. Ignacio stiffens and walks, sits down at his bench. He takes up as little space as possible.

The Booty has been up on the stage for some time, watching them come in, overseeing how they distribute themselves in the room. Her dress shimmers. She seethes with impatience. Ignacio knows that she always opens the ceremony, but he's never seen it, he's only been told.

This is the first Wybrany anniversary celebration Ignacio has attended.

He looks at the portrait of Mr. Wybrany and tries to feel impressed. The Pole, with his furrowed brow and haughty solemnity, reminds him vaguely of the Headmaster, who now enters the room, nods to the Booty, and settles into the armchair of honor, his giant, hairy hands on the armrests.

The Booty clears her throat, calls for silence several times, sips water from a bottle, *ahems*. She composes herself and waits.

Then she speaks. She speaks of the unseen through what can be seen. Ignacio believes in telepathy and senses that the Booty is using language like a riverbed to transmit subterranean messages. She isn't saying what she seems to say: it's something else, more threatening, less clear. At times it appears she refers to the situation with the absent Special; other times, he thinks she's referring to him, or to his transformation into Gerasim.

He can feel the Advisor's stare trained on the back of his head, the Advisor who blames him for being beaten and not reporting it. On the other hand, the Headmaster doesn't seem to have even registered his presence, which saddens him. Does Gerasim disappear in the crowd?

And there is the rival teacher, in tight black satin, her hair done up. Héctor turns to greet her, makes a forward gesture with his hand. She pretends not to notice, but Ignacio sees her tense.

Everything that happens in the *colich* happens without words. Ignacio covers his ears and it doesn't make any difference.

The rumors spread and the Booty mentions them without mentioning them. Ignacio attempts to cast a psychic web over Héctor, who sits with his legs wide and back hunched. Ignacio sees how the girls watch him from a distance.

Yes, Héctor is handsome.

The fact of Héctor's beauty and the threat posed by the girls have never been so obvious. Ignacio thought it would only be the teacher, at first. But here are the girls, taking turns showing themselves off. There will always be more girls, even if they expel a Special now and then.

Like a gas, an air of mourning seeps through the room. Ignacio doesn't know whether it's his own disenchantment or something outside of him, something that pertains to others, something he doesn't know.

Even the portrait hanging behind the Headmaster appears to change its expression, to go completely blank. The Headmaster doesn't even react as the Booty lists the year's challenges one by one, how they were resolved, and how much good morale is required to overcome problems with perseverance, dignity, and determination.

Ignacio feels trapped by the Booty's words, paralyzed by the look the Advisor gives him, by the looks the girls give Héctor, the looks Héctor gives the teacher but not him.

And he feels afraid, insecure, he almost wishes they would twist his arm again, give him physical pain, real pain, to hold on to.

The Booty concludes her speech. The Headmaster rises, thanks her, says a few words. And the dance begins.

VOMIT

I know Valen throws up at night. I've seen her do it in secret, after gorging on all the leftovers she can get her hands on.

Valen wants to be thin, but she's incapable of breaking the cycle.

Cristi and Marina make fun of her constantly, torpedo her with insults. A hail of words, *fattyflabbyballofgrease*, and others, said like that, all at once.

I also think Valen should lose weight, so sometimes I add to their insults.

It's her mother's fault, her mother who cleans at Wybrany and helps out in the kitchen. She takes food and brings it to our dorm at night. She says it's for all of us.

Cristi claims Valen's mother is a gypsy, that's why she steals, because she doesn't know anything other than stealing.

Valen gets anxious if any of us take the bag, just to see what's inside and maybe swipe something we know she especially wants.

She's so impatient for the food that she shrieks, twists around, tries to hit us or throw the nearest object. Then, as she devours the food, she placates us, smiles, wants to share the bounty.

All of this amused me in the beginning. But now I prefer to go out for a run while the others torture each other.

Once I'm outside, thoughts of Valen's insatiability fade away. The cravings, insults, jabs. That no longer interests me.

Lux crouches on the porch. He's grown very quickly, but he's still a matted, big-headed cub. He runs when I try to catch him. He's right not to trust me. The cat only deigns to be held by *him*, who fondles it all day.

The Advisor and his pet.

This makes me think of Teeny. I stop in front of her window and whistle. She looks out and is at my side in a flash, clinging to my leg.

She came without her coat, shivering and hopping the whole time.

"What's up, Teeny?"

Nothing, nothing's up, nothing's ever up. Teeny is the most boring person in the world. She gives me a damp, beseeching look from behind her glasses. The same look, always.

Mid-March and she still has a cold. I take her by the arm and lead her to the fence. The woods, dark and fragrant, extend on the other side.

I stop and listen to the hoot of the screech owl flying overhead.

"You won't try again, will you?" she quavers.

"No."

The mastiff Cayetana trots over to us, the most useless watchdog ever. I scratch her ears and bury my fingers in her scruff. Teeny backs away. She's frightened.

I think about whether or not she'll keep my secret.

"The Advisor promised to bring me to Cárdenas one day. It's been a month and he still hasn't," I say at last.

Teeny smiles, looks away, says nothing.

"What are you laughing at?" I say. "It's not funny."

She coughs to hide her smile. I can tell she doesn't know what to do. Even as a confidant, she isn't any use to me.

"I wasn't laughing."

Then she goes quiet, waiting, sidelined, as the mastiff licks my hand.

"I should do something to make him keep his promise," I say.

"Do it," she whispers.

"It's something bad. Should I do something bad to make him keep his promise?"

She hesitates.

"No. Not something bad."

She doesn't know how to change the subject. She pretends to stumble so I'll help her up.

I pity her.

I walk her back to her room, the austere building, shadowed in ivy. It's curfew.

Back in our brightly painted ward, I pass the bathrooms on my way to bed. There's Valen on her knees, bent over the toilet.

She doesn't see me. I clear my throat but she doesn't hear me either; her retching drowns me out. I watch her for a moment and that's when—like a revelation—I finally decide to act.

ENCOUNTERS

The Booty walks, her hips swinging with fury. But she's smug, too, and ready for her visit.

She's on her way to the Headmaster's office, a flutter in her chest. Her breathing is ragged, lips dry.

The Headmaster is expecting her and she's running late. That lateness weighs on her and she practically runs down the hallway, holding her skirt in her hands.

But suddenly, glimpsed through a window, the evasive figure of the Advisor leaving the brightly colored dorm with a weary stride and Lux in his arms.

The Booty turns, walks back the way she came. She enters the garden and confronts him.

The Advisor, caught off guard, stops and looks at her in surprise.

He mumbles an explanation. She knows he's lying.

She speaks to him, then, about the limits of his role, appropriate places, the need to keep up appearances.

"I can't believe I have to bring this up with you."

He defends himself. His work takes up his entire day, he performs as needed. He isn't a bureaucrat, calling it a day at three on the dot. He doesn't want to be. He points to Lux and argues:

"I'm trying pet therapy. There's nothing wrong with that."

"But it's nighttime," the Booty says. Then, shouting: "Don't you see? It's nighttime!"

Her back is rigid, her eyes flash, and she's almost forgotten about the Headmaster's office.

She's not aware that her incursion into battle is futile.

She's not aware that in every strategic game, a weaker piece is always available for disposal, nor that the greatest weakness lies in one's ignorance of being weak.

Ignacio, on the bench. He stares at his knees as the others dribble, shoot, pass, head, spit, and curse under their breath, because even in soccer, swearing is forbidden at Wybrany.

The gym teacher follows his lesson plans, sticking to the basics: physical education, discipline over the body and mind, a bit of tennis, golf, swimming. But he has permission to organize scrimmages on Saturday afternoons for interested students. Ignacio went because he saw Héctor was going. He trailed behind him, doubtful and slow, until Héctor turned around.

"Hey, you signing up?"

Yes, Ignacio was signing up, he was signing up to ride the bench because he's not good enough, not strong enough, totally lacking in skill.

The times when he gets subbed in, he does his best, dragging himself through the minutes, praying that no one passes him the ball, ashamed that they never do.

He watches Héctor, who plays intelligently, zigzagging so smoothly, skating on the field. Ignacio squints in concentration, attempts to open telepathic channels.

Héctor has the ball. He dribbles around two players and breaks away, but Iván comes at him from the side, leg outstretched, and both trip and tumble on the wet grass, a spinning windmill of shirts and skins.

Even in the tumult, Héctor's shaved head shines.

Ignacio widens his eyes to see them better. They get up, pat each other, but Héctor is limping. Hand holding his calf, a grimace in the sunshine.

They go to him, circle around him. It's not serious.

Héctor comes off the field, passing Ignacio and looking at him.

Ignacio gets ready to sub in, bouncing on his toes, swinging his arms, feeling his heart beat, out of control.

Was it his telepathy that caused Héctor's injury? Was this what he wanted?

He feels guilty. A usurper. He plays badly, out of respect for Héctor and because he knows no other way.

They lose and everyone blames him. Iván gives him a shove and he staggers, but doesn't fall.

Do the others know what he did? That it's his fault?

He runs to the locker room and locks himself in a stall, his throat burning with fury and shame. Then, three light knocks on the metal door. Héctor's cleats appear below the stall, muddied, laces loose, the large feet he knows so well. The feet of a man, of a hero.

Ignacio opens the door and they look at each other. Héctor smiles, enters, shuts the door behind him. He doesn't break his gaze.

They can hear muffled shouts from the field, laughter, Cayetana's bark, the dog driven so insane by the ball that she has to be tied up during games.

A faucet has been left on and water drips and drips, splashing in the ceramic sink.

The sun is so strong they can almost feel it inside the stall. A glint on the metal cistern, the sheen on the tiled wall revealing marks from the moisture.

Héctor gives him a light slap on the back of his neck and Ignacio knows that he's complicit.

Héctor pulls down his shorts. Ignacio's neck is stiff from not looking down, a self-imposed prohibition.

Héctor's voice. Hoarse, urgent:

"Suck my dick."

A few seconds pass, just a few seconds, and Ignacio bends.

The smacking of his saliva, now, as well as the water, still dripping in the sink, the wet slap of water, an almost joyful song that marks his rhythm, and Ignacio feels sheltered by the metal doors, where no one sees him, no one replaces him, he suddenly has a starring role, the others are on the outside.

A VISIT

The Booty rarely receives visits from parents, except when formalizing a student's enrollment. That's the Advisor's arena. But Teeny's mother insists, and her insistence could become a threat if left unsatisfied.

This small, refined woman has power, lots of power, in addition to a daughter she must defend and push to the front, with the other girls.

She smoothes her skirt, sits down, rejecting the offer of tea. Then she speaks:

"She tells me she's always with the . . . scholarship girls."

"There's nothing wrong with that. We're strong proponents of integration," the Booty says.

"Don't misunderstand me. I have no problem with that. It's one of the school's greatest merits. But I do wonder: why her?"

"She's free to choose her own friendships. We respect her choices."

Teeny's mother shifts in her chair. She arches her brows, laces and unlaces her fingers. Her voice changes:

"That girl . . . the one who planned the escape . . . do you happen to think she's good company for my daughter?"

"Celia? Oh, Celia, she's not a bad girl. She received a scholarship because of her high IQ. She doesn't have parents. Or rather, she has quite the undesirable mother, shall we say. Celia represents a big accomplishment for the college. Someone like her could never have attained the kind of education we're giving her. She's the clearest embodiment of our project: our elevated, open humanism. Why does it bother you that your daughter spends time with Celia?"

Teeny's mother starts to piece together a response, but the Booty interrupts her:

"The incident you refer to wasn't an escape. It wasn't even an attempt at one, believe me. The girls explained it later themselves.

It was natural curiosity, and had the most logical motivation. The girl wanted to visit her mother. It's absolutely understandable, and it shows she has a good heart. Or do you think people like Celia don't have feelings?"

"I just think that she isolates my daughter from the other girls. She spends more time in Celia's dorm than her own, which is what her father and I pay for."

"I happen to think the opposite is true. Celia saves your daughter from isolation. Your daughter is shy. Celia looks out for her, gives her attention."

The tension is palpable. The air thick. Both women recompose themselves. The Booty smiles, stretches her legs; the mother weighs the situation, where to direct her strategy next.

"Consider this a request," she says at last. "I want her to have friends of her own class."

"But your daughter can go where she likes in her free time. I'll say it again, she's at liberty here."

"Are you telling me that you won't do anything?"

"We'll look out for her well-being, like we do for all the girls. But Wybrany's ideology is based on respect and harmony. Solidarity with the neediest students."

She nods toward the founder's portrait and sighs:

"Are you not aware of Andrzej Wybrany's rules?"

There is adoration in her voice, in the flick of her wrist and her fingers that unfurl toward the painting, as if to summon the energy it exudes.

The mother looks up, plumbing the image's depths.

"Why don't other girls hang around with the scholarship students, then? Why my daughter? Does this *integration* extend only to her?"

She takes several papers from her purse as she speaks. Papers that could be invoices, reports, judicial sentences. Papers with tight printing. The Booty takes them, reviews them carefully. There is almost no change in her expression, save the slight pulse at her jaw as she hands them back. But her voice is different. Very different.

"I can't tell you how much I appreciate this information. Thank you for bringing it to my attention. Upon further consideration, I do believe you are right. Perhaps we do still have certain areas in need of improvement."

She improvises, then. Measures that sound reasonably acceptable to this mother: Teeny will join the girls' Social Club, she will sign up for their activities and spend more evenings with them throughout the week. The visits she makes to the Specials' building will be limited. The idea is to offer her new pathways, open doors. And this way, the relationship between the two groups will be enriched.

"*Enriched*, yes, that's the word," the Booty says.

"Is there any tea left?" the mother asks.

There is tea, but it's cold. Another mother—Valen's—will prepare a fresh pot. A chubby woman, with graying hair and a servile smile. When she turns her back, the Booty motions toward her:

"She has work and her daughter gets an education—our philosophy in action."

Appeased, Teeny's mother agrees.

From the wall, Andrzej Wybrany appears satisfied with the scene.

FRIENDSHIP

They become inseparable. No more beatings for Ignacio, no more insults or shoves or name-calling. He doesn't have time to think about any of that anymore; he's too wrapped up in other things.

Héctor turns out to have a rather unnuanced personality. Flat, stubborn, his predictability is quite comforting: Ignacio always knows how to please him, what's expected, how he will react at any given moment. This knowledge elevates him to a special status: Ignacio becomes untouchable. He hasn't earned the others' respect, but at least the whispers behind his back are *real* whispers now, ones not intended to be heard.

In the evenings, he supplies Héctor with answers to the homework, finishes his technical drawing worksheets, or writes his essays for him. As Ignacio types, Héctor watches, chewing gum with his back against the wall and his feet on the bedspread. He gives Ignacio affectionate little slaps on the back of the neck, pretend punches that don't leave a bruise.

Ignacio's skin is unmarred now, as even the Headmaster observes when Ignacio goes to his office.

"Gerasim, my Gerasim. Things have improved for you, haven't they?"

The greatest proof of friendship comes when Héctor passes him a blank exam in History class. Her back to the class, the teacher is no one's rival, now Héctor makes fun of her, mocks her as he waits patiently for Ignacio to answer the multiple-choice questions.

With each pencil-darkened circle, Ignacio drives a stake into the teacher's chest, into every girl who ever dared to look at Héctor, into every boy who Héctor could possibly show affection for, some distant, imaginary day.

Héctor is his.

Ignacio fills each circle furiously, with pleasure, racking up points for an 'A'. He is singular, superior, chosen from among all the students at the *colich*.

DOUBTS

She's put her clothes back on and now the Booty sits across from the Headmaster as they chat about academic subjects, coldly and without rancor.

They put aside the insults, exhaustion, and disdain. Forget all about it. Once she rolls up her pantyhose and slips on her shoes, the Booty becomes another woman, unrecognizable to the one before. Her tone shifts naturally, like a snake unconsciously shedding its skin. She looks at the Headmaster and they get down to business.

"I must confess: I don't trust the Advisor."

"What do you mean?"

"It isn't clear what, but he's hiding something. Sometimes I think he's been sent here."

"Sent here? From where? What for?"

"I don't know. From some association, maybe. To look for loose ends."

The Headmaster laughs. "An association? What sort of association?"

"Oh, I don't know. One that wants to report us, denounce us."

The Headmaster stands, tugs at the cuffs of his jacket, paces the perimeter of his large office. The sun is just beginning to set; the days are already longer. The last rays of light filter in, creating shadows that blend with his movements, as if several silhouettes of varying size were crossing the walls, up and down, when it's only the Headmaster's rotund figure.

"Are you afraid?" he asks. "Do you think there's something we should be denounced for?"

She stammers. "I don't know what you mean."

"I'm referring to your conscience. Is your conscience clear?"

"Yes."

"Always?"

"Of course. Always."

He sighs.

"The Advisor is not planning to denounce us. There's nothing here that he has any interest in changing. You do well to have such a clear conscience. You shouldn't worry."

The Booty feels the conversation slipping away from her. She presses:

"I think he could blackmail us. I don't know how, but he could. His attitude concerns me. He's too close to the Specials. He visits their building and they go to see him. Celia, especially."

"I know."

"You know? What do you know?"

"I know about their visits."

"And what's your opinion of them?"

He shrugs.

"They obviously have some sort of agreement. But I don't think it interests us. We all have our favorite students."

He says this even though he knows the Booty will find it odd. She objects:

"If you're referring to your relationship with Ignacio, I think that's quite different. I don't understand why you bring him here, or what you see in that dull, weak boy, but that's your affair. It doesn't affect life in the *colich*. The Advisor's situation isn't the same."

The Headmaster raises an eyebrow.

"And why is that?"

"There's something else about his relationship with Celia. It could contaminate things, create false expectations among the students. I think he's abusing his power, manipulating the scholarship girls. I wouldn't rule out a premeditated plan. Who knows to what end."

"Well, such a plan wouldn't be entirely unfamiliar to you, now would it? We all manipulate, in our own way. Furthermore, who says he's the one in control? Maybe the girl wanted a hold on him so she could get something in exchange. These are things you might not understand."

"I think he uses psychology and his supposed interpersonal skills to get where the rest of us can't."

"And what would you have us do? Fire him because he gets on well with a girl?"

The Booty's eyes flash.

"I'd like to know that's at least a possibility."

The Headmaster laughs, slapping his thighs. The Booty watches him, confused. She doesn't understand the joke, not even when he explains the Advisor's immunity to her. Where he comes from, his power, his assured tenure, all tightly knitted.

The Booty doesn't—can't—understand.

"I never believed that would be such a deciding factor."

"Don't forget where you yourself come from. Nobody dropped in here from the sky. It's best for us to put up with each other. Cover one eye and use your other to see. That's my approach."

THE FIELD TRIP

The first cracks between them appear just a few weeks later, on the field trip to the factory.

Manufacturing work is also important, the technology teacher explains. The boys have seen the machines in pictures, a video of them in operation, the industrial uniforms, the impeccable organization of the assembly line. Now they will actually get to see one, a real factory. An image is not reality, the teacher says. An image is simply a select piece of reality, pure artifice.

The bus rattles down the little road that leads away from Wybrany until it reaches the highway, where it continues on, fast and smooth.

The sky is cloudless. The highway, deserted.

The boys don't sing, not today. It's been forbidden. Headphones sit on the armrests. A tinny female voice prepares them for their visit, explains what the city of Vado was and is no longer, what the city of Cárdenas is and will be.

Ignacio sits with Héctor. They chew gum, laugh, elbow each other.

In front of them, there are rows of other boys, their heads sticking straight up above the seats. Still childlike, some of them.

Blunt and muffled, sound from the headphones comes from around their knees. The cords drag on the floor, fall into the aisle. No one is using them.

The teacher sits in the first row and watches the bleached, empty landscape. He isn't keeping his eye on the boys. He eludes his obligation to reprimand them.

The driver is the father of a Special. He too chews gum, and bounces his leg to the beat of some internal music. His son isn't on the bus because he's one grade ahead. He visited the factory last year. It went well.

"You'll escape this, if you're lucky," the father told him.

He was referring to the line of men—Chinese, Moroccan, South American, but mostly Chinese—snaking its way to the cafeteria at lunchtime.

The boy had liked the machines, the assembly line, the sense of rhythm to the work. But he hadn't liked the line of men.

The driver prefers the bus to that line, as well. From the bus, the landscape unfolds on either side as he drives by. There's no landscape in the factory, and the driver likes watching the sun shimmer on the asphalt horizon like a puddle of water, never to be reached.

He clears his throat to speak to the teacher, but senses his absorption and keeps silent.

In the back of the bus, Héctor chatters away and Ignacio listens. Héctor takes a cigarette from his shirt pocket, lights it, and shares with Ignacio. Two drags for Héctor, one for Ignacio, and there is just enough smoke in the air for all the others—all except the teacher—to turn their heads to look.

Here comes the Goon down the middle of the bus, hips knocking into the seats. He pats Ignacio on the shoulder: they're friendly like they've never been before. He squats—he barely fits in the aisle—and takes out a piece of hash. Ignacio doesn't get it, doesn't know what it is. He doesn't understand why Héctor widens his knees, raises his voice, pushes him to the side so the Goon can sit down.

Now Ignacio is standing, swaying between the seats.

He watches what they do, and it slowly starts to make sense.

He doesn't ask questions. He just watches, trying to memorize so he'll know how to behave in the future.

They give him a hit. They hand him the joint but he isn't sure how to hold it. He takes a drag and inhales. His eyes water.

The Goon is still in Ignacio's seat. He leans against the seat back, spreads his legs, makes himself comfortable. Ignacio knows the Goon isn't planning to leave. He'll have to find another seat.

Ignacio looks to Héctor and mumbles an unintelligible request for assistance.

But Héctor's eyes are half-closed. He smiles, saliva accumulating in the corners of his mouth, pooling as the effects of the hash kick in.

Ignacio turns and limps away, looking for the spot the Goon abandoned.

Iván sees him coming and puts his leg up on the seat.

He taunts him:

"Not your seat."

"We switched. It's mine now."

Iván laughs, pretends like he's about to spit, staring at Ignacio with his leg outstretched, toes pointed at his stomach.

Ignacio looks back, desperate, but Héctor's eyes are still half-closed in a pleasurable stupor.

So Ignacio keeps walking, says *excuse me,* and sits in the only empty seat. Next to the teacher.

Both pretend they don't notice what is happening.

AT NIGHT

I want to talk to Teeny alone, but they make her come with someone else now. She arrives with Julia and Aurori and already they're causing quite a stir.

They peer into our room and sniff around. Not Teeny: she knows it like the back of her hand, and anyway she'd rather sit on the sidelines. She isn't one to pry.

They seem surprised that our beds are the same as theirs, that we have colorful curtains, desks, a nightstand per person.

The only difference is that the Normals have three girls to a room and we have four, plus all the colors, too, which change things.

They sit on the rug and gossip.

I signal to Teeny, but she pretends not to notice, or maybe she really doesn't. She sniffles and listens to the conversation but doesn't join in. I stop trying to get her attention.

Valen, Cristi, and Marina are crazed with excitement. It's something new, the other girls coming here. It makes them proud. Before, we had to be allowed into their spaces, when and how they wanted. Both sides snubbed each other, but today everything is easier, clear and diaphanous, just when nothing matters to me anymore.

I feel dirty.

I watch and despise them. They talk about boys, clothes, brands; they criticize other girls, the teachers, the Booty; they describe their parents' lives—lives which are no longer theirs—the houses, the gardens; they reproduce their parents' fears, their desires.

What do they know about anything?

Do they know even one one-hundredth of what I know?

Has what's happening to me happened to them?

A new force beats in my chest and in part it's a kind of pride. Something about this dirtiness is gratifying, the feeling that I'm now a few steps ahead.

Teeny looks up at me, but she doesn't catch on.

She only knows the little I was able to tell her, which is plenty, but she doesn't understand anything.

I leave and head outside, onto the grounds. I wait for an answer. The lights in the dorm rooms go dark one by one, like blinking eyes.

But it's not a code. It doesn't mean a thing.

A CLASS

The Advisor sits on the table when he teaches, something the other teachers never, ever do. He crosses one leg, letting the other hang; he doesn't use books, he likes the Socratic method, even though he doesn't question the students directly. He either lets them do the asking, or poses questions no one shows any interest in answering.

He's teaching the girls today and wants to talk to them about single-sex education, but Celia, her eyes feverish and glassy, interrupts him:

"Sir, why don't you ever sit in a chair, like the others?"

The girls look at her, scandalized, relishing the inappropriateness of her remark. Always showing off, they whisper, she never stops.

Without moving a single muscle of his face, the Advisor smiles and answers:

"I prefer the table."

"But we're not allowed to sit on our desks."

"Of course you are," he says.

The girls are initially confused, but then they start to climb up onto their desks; first the most daring girl, then they all do it, watching the Advisor out of the corner of their eyes all the while. Some sit on top of their books, creasing the pages. A few notebooks fall on the floor. Pens and erasers. No one picks them up. The commotion quickly dies down.

The Advisor introduces the day's topic in an orderly fashion, following the script written in his notebook, until Valen interjects without raising her hand. She's sucking on a piece of candy.

"But what do you mean by single-sex? I don't get it . . ."

"Our education system here at Wybrany. The fact that boys and girls study separately."

Strategies, cognitive maturation, pilot studies: the Advisor argues in favor of the system but no one listens to him; the girls only fall silent when his tone turns interrogative and he addresses them directly.

"What do you think? Does this system seem good to you? Or are there better alternatives?"

They don't answer. They yawn and swing their feet. He doesn't stop. He looks at them one by one, questioning them with his eyes, smiling the whole time.

Julia, in her shrill voice:

"I think we're more protected this way. The boys are so awful."

Celia replies:

"They're awful because they aren't used to us. If we spent more time together, they'd know how to treat us."

Julia argues:

"Yeah, well you don't even care if they say stupid stuff—you probably like it."

The Advisor lifts his hand, calls for quiet.

"Just a minute, just a minute. Julia has brought up a very interesting concept. She said that you girls are more 'protected' this way."

The strident ringing of the bell brings the class to a close. Given their new position on top of the desks, the girls can't stand up but rather have to sit back down in their seats.

The Advisor doubles down.

"Protection," he insists. "Julia spoke of protection."

He doesn't notice Celia's eyes, violent and wild. Teeny can see her, but he doesn't; he's too absorbed in his talent for persuasion.

Protection as a concept, he says, a concept we will discuss further next class, protection and security versus freedom: is that choice even possible today? How do the scales tip in either direction?

"Is it better to be free and vulnerable or protected but under control? I'll leave it there until next class. Think about it."

Then they get up and go. The Advisor watches them as they exit one after the other. Celia, the last to leave, stares at the tile floor.

He goes only after they've all left the room.

SCORN

He was only occasionally replaced, at first. But lately, Ignacio is often left out of Héctor's plans and returns to his prior place.

He offers himself constantly so as not to lose him completely, but Héctor has grown tired of Ignacio and is looking for a successor.

One night, Héctor is in the middle of a group of new friends. Plans are being hatched right in front of Ignacio, no attempt to hide it. Ignacio hears the whispers, the stifled giggles. He hangs around, waiting to be included, but the rest are tight-lipped. There's only the muffled laughter, the jostling of elbows, something amorphous that he isn't a part of. Ignacio senses their scorn.

"This isn't your thing, kid," Héctor tells him. "Better for you not to be involved. You can't run like the rest of us."

He ruffles Ignacio's hair, a common display of affection toward the littler kids, though Ignacio is only a year younger.

He curses his limp and moves away.

Still, he watches as they put something in their pockets, little baggies, lighters, small, unidentifiable packets.

Ignacio doesn't know. He has a limp and he doesn't know what they're up to, he can't know.

He hobbles back to his room, eyes narrowed, and for the first time in a long while, he starts to feel angry.

The anger is white, blind, it stings his eyes. But it's also a refuge, now that he's alone.

He imagines Héctor with the others, locking themselves behind the heavy metal doors to smoke. He imagines him with his pants down, the hoarse voice:

"Suck my dick."

Ignacio tosses and turns on the bed. He's on the verge of weeping, but plays it off, swallows his anger down his burning throat.

He considers the possibility of snitching, of telling the Headmaster during his next visit, but he doesn't know exactly what to say or how to say it. Gerasim is passive; he rarely speaks. And ultimately, it isn't even that he wants to get Héctor in trouble. What he wants is to be included in all his plans, forever.

Forever.

Ignacio is suffering.

He only asks not to be excluded, not to be left out.

He lays face down and covers his head, a pillow pressed over his ears. Even so, he hears them running down the hall, excited and nervous.

Ignacio was only ever meant for the bathroom, for idle times, for consolation.

You can't run like the rest of us.

It dawns on him at last, in his own way.

I did tell Teeny, but she didn't know what to say, or couldn't fathom it.

She still has a runny nose, her permanent cold, even though it's almost summer. She looks at me with glassy eyes.

Poor Teeny, she can barely take care of herself, but I tell her nevertheless. I tell her, emptying myself.

I tell her what Cárdenas is like, the neighborhood where my mother lives now, which is on the outskirts and is like my old neighborhood, only much dirtier, noisier.

Teeny listens, but she doesn't get, can't get what I'm telling her.

We're out in the hallway so we can be alone. She looks drained.

I suggest we go sit outside where no one will see us, on the front steps of the Specials' ward. The mastiff Cayetana follows us and, as usual, laps my hand.

The other girls and their grating laughter stay behind, inside.

With a single gesture, I try to explain the roar of the streets.

The noise, crowds, lack of space. I had forgotten but now it all comes back, with a few subtle differences.

My mother shares a room with another woman, in an apartment shared with any number of other women.

They almost all work cleaning houses. Two take care of sick people, and one—my mother lowers her voice when she tells me—is a whore. They do what they have to because the power and water could get shut off without warning and they're women who like to wash themselves every day and live with electricity, not in the dark like rats.

There are a lot of whores in the neighborhood, actually. Pimps and clients that pass by in their cars, the windows closed, prepared to unroll them just a crack, only if there's a dish to their liking on the sidewalk.

Teeny blushes when I tell her this. She squirms on the step and I know she must understand some of it, or at least that she's listening and can imagine.

Too many people there, too many.

The puddles are dirty as soon as the rain stops because there was already filth in the street from before. Needles, bits of food, broken, gutted objects.

In the winter it's very cold and very hot in summer.

My mother tells me all of this so I won't go back. You're better off at the *colich,* she says, can't you see?

Meanwhile, he waits outside, driving around the blocks of dingy brown apartment buildings, tiny balconies stuffed with junk and clothes hung on the line.

How to tell her?

Yes, how to tell Teeny, because Teeny is not my mother and won't have the same reaction. My mother rejects what I say, even rebels against it in her own way—shaking her head, her eyes damp—but I fear that ultimately she accepts it as the lesser evil.

Wybrany is a lesser evil. Not even an evil, in fact. A stroke of luck.

This is what she thinks. Maybe she's right and I don't know how to see it.

He seems nervous on the ride back, anguished somehow. Sadness swamps his retinas and they ache. He rubs his eyes. He feels both discomfort and contentment, from all he's seen and that he's lucky enough not to have to see it every day. I know this because he tells me himself, his hand on my thigh, and I tell Teeny, and she nods slightly, understands now. Maybe.

Okay, I tell him, maybe not every day, but sometimes. I want to come again.

Come becomes *go* as the kilometers bring us closer to Wybrany. I appeal to him the whole ride, and I know how to make my plea a demand.

The request becomes a commercial transaction: when I give him something, I can demand a price. Negotiate or blackmail in exchange.

"So you'll go back?" Teeny asks, staring straight ahead.

"Yes."

I'll go back every chance I get, as often as possible.

So I don't forget where I come from.

THE SUB

They're playing a better team today, kids who are just a little older.

Ignacio is on the bench, waiting to go in. He swings his feet, observes his surroundings. Héctor doesn't look at him anymore. Ignacio doesn't even hope for it. He scrapes at the dirt with the toe of his cleats. The sun warms his bare legs, now darkened by straight, soft hair.

He looks at the other team, on the other bench.

There is another boy, a boy like the one he used to be. An outcast. A year older, sure, but hardly any taller, big-boned, brown hair parted to the side, round glasses, and a jutting bottom lip. Ignacio is watching him. The other boy looks down, averting his eyes.

Ignacio stares at him and stops scuffing the dirt. The other boy, motionless, keeps his eyes on the ground. Ignacio concentrates on him, he sends signals, gives him an order. The boy looks up and sees him. Blushes.

Other boys run up and down the field, they pant and sweat, but the boys on the bench don't see them: the players have become gauzy, distant.

The air clots.

Ignacio thinks about how the others don't really know him. It's time to surprise them, set a new tone.

The mastiff barks in the distance, the chain chafing her neck, sweeping dust from side to side as she lunges after the ball.

The air grows thicker. It's dust, it's the telepathy, the transmissions between the two boys on the two benches.

The boy's name comes back to him: Rodrigo. A Special, one of those kids the others pay to do their assignments. He's good at math and physics, disciplined and quiet. Ignacio used to do other kids' work, too. Though all of that stopped a while ago.

The boys look at each other, and the spectre of Héctor disappears.

The game plays on, a corner kick results in a goal, the goal in a scuffle, someone touched the ball with his hand. The teacher intervenes. There's an argument and Ignacio momentarily loses focus.

When he turns his attention back, Rodrigo is no longer on his bench. Ignacio sees him in the distance, heading toward the locker room, shorts rippling in the warm breeze, thin legs and an uncertain stride, like he's in a hurry, or afraid.

Ignacio goes after him. The walk to the locker room is all confusion in his ears: the sounds of the game now faraway, the dog's bark, the teacher's voice calling to him, telling him to hurry up, the sub always has to be ready to go in.

He positions himself in front of the metal door and knocks. He's careful to make sure his shoes stick under, invade the stall, so the other boy will recognize the gesture and understand.

It's not how he imagined. Rodrigo won't open the door. Instead he asks:

"What's up? What do you want?"

Ignacio is unsure of his next move. He hesitates briefly and Héctor's voice swells in his temples, those words that echoed with authority. Ignacio says *open up* but he thinks *suck my dick,* he has to insist several times, increasingly urgent, until the other boy slides the latch and looks out at him, confused.

Ignacio pushes him back inside with a violence that is unfamiliar. Rodrigo's mouth makes sounds of protest, but a punch silences him.

Ignacio hits his nose, his lips, stomach, he punches him, insults him at the same time. Rodrigo just cries, he doesn't defend himself.

Another goal, they both hear the cheers, and that's when Ignacio pulls down his shorts and hollows out his voice, makes it as hoarse as possible, as close as possible to that other voice. He gives the command.

SUMMER

May marches on, then June. There are more visits and each time the contrast between the two worlds grows deeper every time.

They have to leave late at night because the days are long and they must go in secret. When they arrive, they are greeted by the spectacle of darkness in both the people and things.

The looks that pass between mother and daughter have little to say now, and serve as little more than recriminations for their mutual disinterest.

The mother doesn't ask how it is that her daughter is able to leave the *colich,* or who brings her. She might prefer not to know. This hurts Celia.

"You don't want to know anything about my life. Does this all seem normal to you?"

Skinny, wrinkled, the mother scratches her scalp and doesn't attempt an answer. Her mouth twitches in a way that repulses Celia. She looks at the mother's straw-like hair, unkempt, the dark roots. Her hands, ruddy and swollen. The dirty tracksuit.

"You should take care of yourself. You'll never get a better job like this."

The mother responds, nonplussed:

"My, my aren't you the little lady."

"It's not about being a 'lady,' mamá. You've let yourself go."

She gestures to the room: pots and pans piled in the sink, grease stains on the walls. The mother turns to her.

"You haven't tried the flan."

"I don't want to. I saw that your milk was expired."

"The milk's not bad. What are you talking about? No one around here has died from drinking it."

"I didn't ask you to make me a flan. There are plenty of flans back at the *colich.*"

"Okay, then. Fine. Sorry. I just wanted to make you happy."

"If you wanted to make me happy, you wouldn't have left me there. I didn't want to leave. A flan won't fix the fact that you abandoned me."

But her reproach is no longer valid.

And she knows it.

Her perspective has changed and she's starting to see things in a different light.

Circumstances that were once commonplace are now tinged with repulsion and pity. What was worn out before is now filthy. Accumulation has become hoarding.

For the first time, Celia is beginning to have the sense that she's been saved. She feels a faint gratitude, a fear she could lose her privilege.

She still doesn't want to forget, but her thoughts of escape are dissipating.

Sentimentality—once fanned by distance and separation—cedes to a routine of the *already-seen,* and the discomfort of returning to see it again.

And so the transactions start to lose their meaning, and become nothing but torn flesh, pure guts.

BEHIND

Teeny goes looking for Celia, whom she hasn't seen in two days.

Valen stuffs a pastry under her pillow. With a mouth full of crumbs, she reports:

"She's sick. She doesn't want to talk to anyone."

Teeny approaches the lump in the bed, the crumpled body. She says nothing, just stands there, waiting.

Behind her, Valen mumbles:

"Where are Julia and Aurori? What are you doing here by yourself? You know you're not allowed to come alone."

Teeny doesn't answer. She simply coughs and stands beside the bed, observing Celia's head, her curved back, the whole of her closed off, silent.

Valen finishes eating in secret and then goes to throw up, look for more food, or both. Teeny takes her chance and leans over Celia, speaking softly:

"Did you go back to Cárdenas? Did something happen?"

"Leave me alone."

This hurts her, but Teeny doesn't reply. She looks for a spot to sit and settles behind Celia, curled against her, patient, expecting nothing. Celia rolls over and looks at her with loathing.

"I told you to leave me alone. You have no idea what's wrong with me," she spits. "You have no idea and you never will. What happened to me will never happen to you."

"Why not?" Teeny whispers.

"Because you're lucky. They don't want you."

Celia's been crying and her lips are slightly swollen. Teeny looks at her, frightened: Celia seems bigger somehow, stronger, more powerful, despite the pain and tears. Teeny doesn't argue with her, or even move. She waits as Celia finishes ticking off her insults one by one.

They are silent. And for a moment, their eyes meet.

CHILDHOOD

The Headmaster answers the door, nose still burning from the cocaine. Ignacio folds his hands behind his back and waits patiently for permission to enter.

"I wasn't expecting you just now, Gerasim, but no matter. Has something happened?"

Ignacio walks in without a response, turns in a circle, taking in the Headmaster's room, the fortress that is denied to others but which Ignacio is allowed to enter. He feels a sudden twinge of invulnerability.

He sits down on the sofa, waits for the Headmaster to come to him.

He commands it with a look, a taunt dancing in his eyes.

The Headmaster moves in close, looks down at him, tugs at his goatee with satisfaction.

"You're changing, Gerasim. I think you're starting to leave boyhood behind."

Ignacio smiles. Yes, it's true. He's no longer a boy. He clears his throat.

"Would you like me to read you something, sir?"

That's all he says. The Headmaster hands him a magazine, pointing to an article on extinguished cities. He sinks into the armchair, closes his eyes, and waits.

Ignacio reads.

Halfway through the article, without changing his posture, without opening his eyes, the Headmaster interrupts him:

"When that dying man in the story thinks about the happy times in his life, he realizes that everything he had once enjoyed—wealth, good food, trips, the praise of his subordinates—all of that no longer appeals to him. Only memories of his childhood are able to give him an authentic feeling of happiness. Childhood: the very thing that is lost to us forever."

Ignacio looks up, considers this a moment.

"I don't have a single good memory from my childhood. I'm just starting to feel happy now."

"I know. I know that," the Headmaster says. "I just wanted to hear you say it."

He asks Ignacio to come closer so he can stroke his hair. Ignacio goes to him, knowing that—this time—he can choose whether or not to be stroked.

THEY MEET

Celia is still there, at the welcome party for new students held in late June. She's there with the others but apart from them, and that's when she tells Teeny about disappearing, about doing it despite the fear, pain, and doubt.

Celia speaks like never before, quickly, stumbling over her words. She'd never felt the need to be understood, just the need to talk, but now that her time is almost up she wants to say everything as clearly as she can.

The new students enter, the first years, boys and girls eleven, twelve years old. Their parents sit proudly, watching them with relief, with the feeling that they've done what is right, they've sacrificed for them, bankrupted themselves if necessary.

These kinds of conversations abound, filling the air with long, resonant words: sacrifice, transformation, well-being, security, investment.

Summer is just beginning: yellowing grass, muffled cricket song from the woods. Chairs have been arranged in the garden and huge sun umbrellas shade the guests.

The new arrivals run around like little children, leaving prints of crushed grass with every step.

No one reprimands them. It's a special day. An exception has been granted.

The children look happy, but apprehensive. They'll be leaving their parents for some time, which perhaps means forever.

Some mothers cry, the fathers' chins tremble, but their decision is firm. They know that the future depends on this separation.

The tall poplars and Eastern hemlocks surrounding Wybrany oversee the farewells, impassive. There's barely a breeze and the air is stifling, the customary stillness of summer.

Night falls, the speeches end, and the Specials' mothers—decked out in well-starched aprons and bonnets—serve cocktails and a light, healthy supper composed primarily of vegetables and cheeses. The other mothers wear sleeveless dresses, the fathers wear their jackets, and the Booty strolls among them, feeling beautiful on this night.

The Headmaster mingles as well, but sparingly, never breaching the boundary that keeps him removed from the rest.

At the edge of the gathering, Celia and Teeny aren't eating, aren't drinking. The Advisor watches them from afar as he feeds Lux thin slices of smoked salt cod. He isn't yet aware, doesn't yet know, and so is relaxed as he watches them. Contented, even.

The girls sit on the grass, illuminated by a solar-powered lamppost that spills faint bluish light over them, as if they'd been briefly dipped in diluted ink.

Celia is telling her about another party. There were two more men, and she was the draw. The Advisor enjoyed himself even before he participated. Teeny chews her lip. She understands.

It's hard for Teeny to speak, but she dares to, at last. So quietly that Celia has to ask her to repeat herself.

"Can't you say no?" she repeats.

Celia laughs, her teeth tinged by the light. A deep belly laugh.

"I'm not even sure whether I like it or not!"

Celia stands and smoothes her dress, shedding little blades of grass. Teeny doesn't like seeing her laugh, not this time. She stands up next to her, close to Celia's body.

"You don't mean that," she says.

"I don't know. I don't know anything. I don't know what I'm going to do. But I have to leave."

Celia tries not to cry. She doesn't want the Advisor to see that.

"Will you go back to your mother?"

"No, somewhere else. I'm not sure where."

"So you're leaving me alone, then?" Teeny says.

Celia stares. She doesn't try to console her. She wouldn't know how. She could tell her that she'll find another friend, she could tell her that Valen needs help, that she knows how to listen. She could tell her that there's always the mastiff, that she should get over her fear of the dog. She could lie to her once, many times, but she doesn't say a word.

They simply stand there for a moment, motionless, and watch the shadow of a boy walking away, one of the new kids, still small, skinny. He looks out of place, walking by himself, with a little limp. He seems to be looking for a secluded place to sit, fleeing some taunt, a shove.

A woman, his mother, calls to him:

"Ignacio!"

The shadow turns.

The cry of a screech owl swoops over them. Celia lifts her head and listens. She hears its message.

THE SEAT

The new school year has just begun and her seat is empty. It's been empty all week, almost since the first day of class, and the blank space is an accusation. Teeny knows that Celia isn't sick, the others all know it, too. But no one asks, no one says a word.

French class is about to begin when the door opens and the Booty stalks in, asking permission as she makes her way through the rows of desks without waiting for an answer. She stands at the podium, smoothes her blouse, observes the girls, and speaks.

She doesn't talk about Celia, but she makes it clear that an absence is always a response to something. And she makes it especially clear that this is a permanent absence.

She employs the usual symbols—caged birds, weeds that hinder the nourishment of rosebushes, clouds that block the sun: a whole apparatus of lifeless nature she navigates with ease. And yet there is a tremor behind her words. An anxious fury, and this is strange.

The girls whisper, handing the words between them under their breath. A hum spreads like a net through the classroom.

Expulsion. They expelled her.

Only Teeny looks straight ahead. She doesn't make a sound, doesn't receive or pass on the rumors. Her empty eyes betray no confusion, just a hint of powerlessness. The Booty doesn't look at her, nor does the French teacher. No one pays her any attention, no one is worried. She never guessed anything before and she's not a threat now, either.

"What do you think she did?"

"I saw it coming."

"Took them long enough."

"I feel bad for her."

"But when did it happen?"

Those words sound and swell as the Booty takes her leave and stomps from the room with an angry, exaggerated swagger. The teacher calls for quiet but the conversations rumble in the background, even though the class goes on in spite of it all, conjugations, prepositions, *le vocabulaire . . .*

They ask Teeny:

"What happened? You must know something. Tell us."

It's dawned on them that she could have information, but Teeny doesn't speak, Teeny never speaks. And certainly not in the middle of class.

Like always, she looks back at them with damp eyes. Like always, she blows her nose and remains silent.

"NEVER MORE THAN TWO HUNDRED"

The questions continue after class, and spill over into the following days, all kinds of indirect, sinuous questions. Teeny is stubborn in her silence. Not because she doesn't want to talk but because she doesn't know what she should say, or how.

It's a serious problem, the Booty thinks as she observes the Advisor, who these days walks around the *colich* with a smile frozen on his face.

The Booty only thinks about this occasionally. Not when she's naked, balancing on high heels before the Headmaster. But a half hour later, dressed again in her tailored suit, legs crossed, she confronts him.

He dismisses her concerns.

"The best way to avoid chaos is by controlling it: lock it up in a pen and feed it separately," he says.

He tells her there are too many girls in the world. The absence of one of them is not that important. There are still more urgent affairs they must attend to. A new student application has been submitted, he explains, though the school year is already underway.

"The boy was held back," the Booty says after hearing the details. "We never planned to allow for this type of admission."

"He's the son of a government minister. We don't have a say."

"An ex-minister," she says. "He was removed two months ago."

"*Ex* is just a prefix. Two letters don't mean a thing. You're too rigid."

"If we don't stem the tide, Wybrany will be filled with exceptions. The rules clearly establish that repeating students will not be admitted. And that the number of places must always be fixed."

"The rules aren't inviolable. We made them, they didn't come from the heavens. And besides, there *is* an opening at present."

The Booty widens her eyes, blinks.

"Celia? This boy would take the place of a girl, a Special?"

"Not her place. But her number, yes. The total count won't change. That's what you want, isn't it? When they ask how many students we have, we can always give a round figure. *Never more than two hundred*, that's your motto."

Yes, that's her motto. They study the application, the handwriting that slants slightly to the left, running outside the boxes on the forms. The boy's name is Héctor, a hero's name. He'll join the group of first years.

He'll just be a New Kid among the new kids; no one will notice anything.

A meeting is scheduled with his parents right away.

PART TWO

A SUBSTITUTE'S DIARY

SUNDAY, NOVEMBER 12TH

I arrived at the *colich* yesterday. By the time I'd finally found it, night had fallen. I confess: I'm a terrible driver, especially on unfamiliar roads. I made my first mistake at the detour on the highway and had to turn around and start over. Later, I drove down a dirt road through a pine tree forest. I drove slowly, uncertainly. I switched on my high beams, blinding a few rabbits. I heard the cry of a bird. I don't know which kind.

I finally reached the end of the road, hungry and disoriented.

My disconcertion was compounded by the total darkness. Apparently, everyone here turns in early. Silhouettes of stone buildings stood among the shadows. Not as large as I would have expected, but ornate and pretentious, like from another time.

I was met at the gate by a woman wearing an apron, her head bowed. She seemed to expect me because she didn't ask for my name or reason for being there. She simply murmured *follow me* and led me to my room in a stone dormitory building on the left side of the property.

The room is spare but comfortable enough. Double bed, mounted TV, desk with a swivel chair, prints of contemporary art on the wall. I tried the internet connection and it seemed to work fine. I considered taking a shower, but I didn't know where to find the bathroom and the woman in the apron disappeared without giving me any instructions. I put my clothes in the closet and got into bed, still dressed and without any dinner.

Unusual for me, I fell fast asleep.

I can't quite remember it today, but I had a strange dream that kept me engrossed the whole night.

I was awoken this morning by the ringing of a telephone I hadn't noticed on the nightstand yesterday. A cordial female voice summons me to a meeting in one hour. A welcome meeting, she specifies. I look at the clock. It's only 8 A.M, and a Sunday, too. The sun has barely risen. I can see a well-tended garden through the window with tall hedges, the vestiges of the night's fog.

I realize I will have to adapt to a different schedule.

I've peered into the hallway and seen other doors just like mine, but none appear to be to a bathroom. I have no idea where to wash up, do my business. I've been forced to urinate in a plastic bottle, which I've stashed behind the nightstand. I've wiped the sleep from my eyes with a tissue and now I write as I wait for the meeting.

I'll know more soon.

(. . .)

I met Señor J. and I still don't know what to make of him. The headmaster of the *colich* looks more like a shareholder than a head of school. It's hard to explain, but there's something in his air, like a smug businessman instead of someone responsible for educating the young. A self-satisfied, relaxed man: pleasant expression, deep, confident voice, a graying goatee he strokes now and then.

From behind round glasses, he gives me a look that could be either kind or condescending. He shakes my hand and welcomes me enthusiastically. I'm suddenly put at ease.

The assistant headmaster is also at the meeting. Skinny and pale with dark circles under his eyes, he's submissive to Señor J., eager to please. No firm handshake from him, just a limp and noncommittal grasp. He smiles broadly, showing long, yellowed teeth. He's friendly, but it's an awkward friendliness. Fixed eyes, stiff expression. I couldn't tell whether he liked me or not.

Our conversation is brief. I have the impression they both think I know all about the school already, or maybe they don't want to bore me with superfluous explanations early on. They limit themselves to giving me precise instructions. The assistant headmaster gives me a folder with my student files, the notebook of the teacher I'm replacing, a copy of my contract, and a flash drive.

"You start tomorrow," he adds.

I go ahead and ask what happened to the teacher on leave. I need to calculate how long I'll be able to work here, but I don't want to seem rude, so I murmur the question. The assistant headmaster makes a slight, evasive gesture with his hand; I'm not even sure he's heard me.

Things being what they are, I don't press.

Then Señor J. opens one of the large windows, offers me a cigar (which I turn down) and smokes leisurely, leaning against the wall. It's obvious he's scrutinizing me, but I'm not intimidated.

I would have happily accepted a coffee. The sun has risen fully and I still haven't eaten since yesterday afternoon. I worry my stomach is growling. I worry about my bad breath and whether they've noticed it.

What should I do? Ask them where I could get some breakfast around here? What I have to do to take a shower? Brush my teeth?

What I finally do: stand up, thank them, say goodbye, and leave, closing the door behind me. I have the urge to press my ear against the door. Are they discussing me? Or is bringing a new teacher on board just another part of the routine?

I return to my room and put all the material I've received in its place. Then I wait without knowing what for. I wait a good long while. I don't keep track of the time. Maybe an hour, maybe two.

I write in this journal.

My hunger pangs grow stronger, the *colich* fills with sounds. I still haven't eaten. Fortunately, there are more plastic cups in my room. I pee in another one and hide it with the first, which has already started to stink.

Through the window, I see several students heading out to play sports. Impeccable, tidy boys bursting with health, running down the fields with their shiny hair, cheering each other on. Farther away, I make out a group of girls accompanied by a huge, cinnamon-colored dog. I can't see anything else, given both the distance and my nearsightedness.

At the moment, I feel isolated. Isolated and sad.

(. . .)

I'm not sure what I should be doing. Spending the whole day in my room looks bad, but neither does it seem appropriate to introduce myself to colleagues in my current state: disheveled, stomach growling. Besides, wandering around to suss out the situation could look suspicious. And unquestionably, the last thing I want to do is raise suspicion.

Nevertheless, I opt to head out and investigate anyway.

I come across an enormous dining hall with different areas separated by adjustable panels. A sign at the entrance details the menu and hours of operation. Breakfast is finished, but thankfully there are just two hours before lunch. Feeling encouraged, I continue my rounds, killing time. I have the good fortune of finding the student restrooms.

Finally, release.

I explore the hallways, relieved at last, most likely retracing my steps unintentionally.

I exchange hellos with several people, but we don't introduce ourselves.

I don't encounter many people in general; typical Sunday atmosphere at a boarding school. The students who aren't out on the playing fields must be in their rooms, resting or studying. They aren't with their parents. This weekend, the assistant headmaster informed me, is not a visiting weekend.

I eat lunch alone in the section reserved for teachers. I'm served by two aged—but not old—and very quiet women. The meal is exquisite: cream of vegetable soup, smoked ham, the marinated dogfish so typical in this part of the country.

I return to my room. Someone has made the bed and taken the two cups of urine. I'm embarrassed, but glad for the fresh air. I lie down and fall asleep immediately. Two or three hours must pass.

When I wake up, I start reviewing the student files. The teacher's notebook is awash in hasty, untidy notations—crossings-out, scribbles, grease stains. Anxious handwriting compiles details of complete or incomplete exercises, papers submitted, exam grades, opinions, problems, quibbles along the lines of *didn't turn in his homework yesterday, needs to improve spelling, could do better.*

The work seems routine and not very exciting. Just what I need.

I call to have dinner brought to my room. This way, I can look busy. When the staff member arrives with my dinner, there's hardly any room on the table for the tray. He hesitates a moment before setting it on a bench. As soon as he's gone, I stack the papers over on one side and eat while watching TV. Then I pee in a cup and get back in bed.

I can't sleep. I obviously slept too much during the day. I try to read but I can't concentrate. The pages give off an unsettling scent of mothballs; the words dance, leap over each other. My head is spinning, my eyes sting. I'm writing this with dinner's leftovers piled in front of me.

My body is starting to smell. The urine next to the nightstand is polluting the air.

I need to bathe immediately.

MONDAY, NOVEMBER 13TH

I had a sudden revelation. Like I said, I was feeling dirty and desolate, tapping my fingers on the table, when my eyes came to rest on the little side door of a built-in closet.

A built-in closet, I thought. But no.

It was a bathroom, complete with shower stall, sink, and toilet. A whole bathroom, all for me.

I don't know how I didn't see it before.

In fairness, the door is almost invisible—white on white—the crack barely noticeable. But there's a whole world hidden behind it: clean towels, bath products, hair dryer mounted on the wall.

I showered, shaved, and brushed my teeth. I don't think I've ever been happier.

Then I slept like a log until the phone woke me again.

Bad start to the day, bad start. The same female voice (the assistant headmaster's secretary?) informed me that my students were waiting. I was late for class.

I made up an excuse and dashed out, uncombed, sleep in my eyes (again).

I couldn't find the classroom at first. To a newcomer, the *colich* is a labyrinth. The lecture building can be accessed by two opposite-facing doors, but once inside, the symmetry is absolute: the two parts never meet. I later learned this layout is due to the single-sex segregation requirement. The resulting design is extremely detailed:

a ruthless division of a more or less limited space. You need a good memory and understanding of spatial logic in order not to be confused.

Lacking in both those areas, I walked in several circles before finding the door to my first class.

Then it was just a matter of turning the knob and everything going blurry. All I remember from that first instant are dozens of eyes, all locked on me. An attentive silence, the sound of tree branches tapping lightly on the windowpanes, the polished floor, my unease.

It became apparent the students were expecting something of me, but I had nothing to offer.

I introduced myself, muttered vagaries. I knew I had to improvise. Suddenly, an idea: I handed out sheets of paper and told them to write down their most recent dream. Put their names at the top of the page, use their best penmanship, pay attention to the margins.

"Sleep-dream or wish-dream?" they asked me.

"Sleep, sleep, an oneiric dream," I specified.

Some told me they couldn't really remember their dreams. Others couldn't remember if they had dreamt at all.

I told them they could make something up.

One boy said he would make his up regardless; he was embarrassed to tell me the real one.

I gave him permission to do so and they quieted down at last. I began to feel calmer. The scratch of pens on paper, a dog barking in the distance. I looked out the window and there was the mastiff again, running up and down one of the paths with a certain desperation. The dog was a giant.

Given the results—peace and quiet—I did the same thing in the next class, and the next, and the next, until I finished with all four groups I'd been assigned: two classes of boys, and two of girls.

I'm shocked I got through the morning without a serious mistake.

I've realized that being a teacher is easy, in the end. You walk into class, decide what they have to do, and then they do it.

The students wait for instructions, resigned as a herd of livestock—well-tended, comfortable livestock. You might hear a little commotion as you near the classroom door, and when you enter they might look at you with some distrust, but they're always submissive. You speak and they listen. You order and they obey.

I felt better having established this.

But then in the dining hall, I was hit with another wall of anxiety. Several groups of teachers had distributed themselves evenly among the tables. I hesitated. If I chose to sit with some and not others, I'd almost certainly be positioning myself in some way. But, to be honest, no one asked me to join them. Not a single one made any gesture of recognition or friendship. I decided to eat alone.

Then, as I was leaving, I saw the assistant headmaster come in with a pretty teacher, straight-backed, lively, compact. He nodded to me and she fixed her eyes on mine, flashing the hint of a bright smile.

I still have her image in my mind, a lure toward something yet to be determined.

(. . .)

I'm back in my room, and I'm perplexed. What do they do around here in the evenings? Is something expected of me? Something I'm not even aware of?

Slowly, I walk down the gold-trimmed carpeting in the hallway. It's like being in an old hotel, but the walls are all white, the doors don't have moldings, and the general vibe is more like a hospital than a school. My room is at the very end. I listen for sounds from behind the neighboring doors.

Nothing.

I'll spend the evening in my room. I can't think of a better option.

Piles of graph paper covered in my students' dreams and nightmares are spread out on the table.

What should I do with all this? Just read them, make corrections?

Can dreams be corrected?

One paragraph jumps out: *We lived in an enormous chalet surrounded by the sea. We were happy. One day, the world became just as small as if it were draining away down a funnel.*

The image is seductive. This could be my own dream, although—strictly speaking—I've never had a chalet by the sea.

TUESDAY, NOVEMBER 14TH

After another morning just like the day before, I've been called to a meeting of the education team. The same phone, ripping me from sleep—this time during my *siesta*. The same voice, that secretarial voice that sets me on edge.

The *education team*. I'm not really sure what an education team does. It sounds sporty, dynamic. Personally, I'm really rather passive. I prepare my folder with the student information sheets and spend the next two hours marking the assignments. I'll bring them with me, just in case.

They're notable, the compositions. For one thing, the kids have a good command of writing: vocabulary, syntax, narrative strategies. Moreover, they have very strange dreams. They frequently live in houses that *are* but *aren't*, with parents who *are* but *aren't*, in a school that *is* but *isn't*. Chases, murders, talking objects, impossible landscapes of sea, desert, mountains.

Everything in the dreams could exist, but never does.

One girl wrote: *I dreamt of you even before I knew you had come to the school.* Her name is Irene. I memorize it.

I don't assign grades. Some comments, sure, on spelling, etc. . . . I prefer not to comment on style. I firmly believe in freedom.

I put all the papers in my folder and leave for the meeting. Inevitably, I get lost again.

I ask a group of students stretched out in the courtyard for directions. I sense their disdain when they point to the building on the right side of the school, a stone building with large windows and exterior moldings, covered in jasmine: purely imported English design. The meeting room is in the back. At a near sprint, I make it just on time.

I'm panting when I open the door. The assistant headmaster is there with a handful of teachers, all seated around a glass table. Everyone has a laptop except me. I decide not to consider it a disadvantage, but rather as a sign of character, of strength. I look for an open seat, set my folder on the table, and face them.

The assistant headmaster looks tired. He rubs his eyes, smiles and speaks. "Before we continue, perhaps we ought to introduce ourselves."

They all nod and take turns standing up. I'm surprised once again by the *colich*'s discipline, its efficiency. Every action appears to be ruled by a series of steps so exacting a newcomer could never get them right. And yet, there's a graciousness toward mistakes, a constant impression of affability. I'm blanketed in smiles and pleasant words. The same people who kept their distance in the dining room are now falling all over themselves in exaggerated cordiality.

This makes me even more uncomfortable.

There are many teachers and none really stand out: just a meld of faces, names, and subjects. But as I write, a certain Martínez comes to mind, a science teacher who almost broke my fingers while shaking my hand. Chubby and vigorous, probably close to retirement. I don't know why, but he has a sort of paternalism that draws me to him. I've always liked to be looked after. I had seen the math teacher, Ledesma, in the dining room already: young, thin, a long, straight mustache and thick brows, always looking at the floor or off to the side. Sacramenta is another singular character, but this is due to her size: she's excessively overweight, dark-haired, with an extravagant smile. She teaches History. She tells me to call her Sacra, an unpleasant-sounding nickname that reminds me of *sacrum*, or *acrid*.

The pretty teacher who smiled at me yesterday comes over from the other side of the room and plants a kiss on each of my cheeks. She says her name, Marieta, and our eyes lock. Moments after she's gone, I can still smell lilacs.

I introduce myself by my last name, given that this seems to be the custom among the men.

"Bedragare." But then I add, "Isidro Bedragare."

Sacra furrows her brow. *Italian?* she asks. No, no, nothing like that. I hasten to explain further, but the assistant headmaster indicates that this is unnecessary. Despite his smile—or perhaps because of it—I read impatience in his movements, a disapproval of the interruption.

Message received.

To make up for it, I concentrate on listening to everyone carefully, even though I don't understand much.

The meeting is—I suppose—a normal teachers' meeting. They discuss programming, performances, executive planning, bilingualism, rules, well-adjusted students and students on their way to becoming adjusted. I don't believe I heard the words *children, class, lesson,* or *exam.* Nor *composition,* to my disappointment.

Marieta is by far the most organized of the group. She constantly shares ideas, listens, shuffles papers, makes arguments, types, suggests, advises.

She and the assistant headmaster are a team. This quickly becomes obvious.

I'm out of my element.

At some point, I must have a look of shock on my face because several teachers offer to clear up my doubts despite the fact that I haven't expressed any.

I simply thank them. I don't say anything about the compositions. I don't even open the folder.

Several times, I'm afraid of giving myself away. My lack of teaching experience should be obvious, but maybe I can hide it by staying quiet, going with the flow, doing what they do, smiling and expressing my concerns at the right time.

The effort required to fake all this is exhausting, but absolutely crucial.

At least as long as this substitute job lasts. A long time, I hope. As long as possible.

THURSDAY, NOVEMBER 16TH

Today was my fourth day at the *colich,* my fourth day of classes. A routine is slowly taking shape. I'm hopeful that discipline and order will come next, and then everything will be cyclical, steady living, no worries.

I teach in the mornings and cover study hall or go to meetings in the afternoon. They continue to request my presence by phone when I least expect it, but now I'm managing to not be late or show up in the wrong place. I usually sit near Martínez, the only person who seems to recognize me as part of the group. He pats me on the shoulder, smiles kindly; I think he looks at me with pity, or compassion.

Marieta also attends the meetings, but her professional bearing throws me off my game. I haven't managed to talk to her directly, don't even understand what it is she does at the *colich*. I don't speak her language. Unfortunately, we don't have the same lunch period either, and every time I leave the dining hall, she's coming in. She greets me with a smooth wave and a quick smile, and that's it.

"What does that woman teach?" I ask a student in the hallway.

The boy is chewing gum—against the rules—and answers without meeting my eye:

"She's not a teacher."

"Oh? What does she do, then?"

"She's the counselor."

Ah, I see. I've heard of them: adolescent psychologists, spiritual advisors, a kind of mentor, a steward of communal living. I'm pensive. So that's what drives her to be so systematic, so attentive to every small shift in the psyche. I wonder if she's already diagnosed me.

The boy stares at the floor, chewing.

"Spit out that gum."

It's the first time I've exercised my authority. I surprise myself. The boy takes the gum out of his mouth, wraps it in a piece of paper, and puts it in his pocket.

The kids aren't badly behaved. They generally accept the hierarchy and don't complain, don't talk back. This makes me feel more confident in my masquerade.

In class, everything revolves around their compositions and dreams. It's going well; it's easy and leaves me with plenty of free time. I do slight variations (I'm not very imaginative), such as forcing them to use certain words or narrate from different viewpoints (a character in a dream, a dream interpreter, even a fortune-teller making a prediction). Sooner or later I'll run out of prompts, but I'll wring what I can from them as long as they last.

This morning, a girl interrupted me as I was assigning a new exercise:

"The other teacher explained things in the book to us. We didn't write as many compositions."

I believe *things in the book* refers to pronouns, articles, direct and indirect objects, that sort of thing.

"I'm the teacher," I answer.

But that's not true. Someone else is the teacher. I'm just a substitute.

Even so, I don't give in:

"Include the words: *vomit, piglet, interstellar, tamed, tank*."

I watch as they consult their dictionaries, scratching their pens across the sheets of paper I hand out and later collect to bring back to my room, where I let them pile up in a corner of my desk.

I've figured out who Irene is. Sharp expression, a know-it-all. She looks at me sideways, as I do her. She has a lazy eye with a twitchy lid. I think she even wears glasses with clear lenses to hide it.

She still includes ambiguous innuendos in her work, but they're so subtle I can hardly admonish her for it. Unfortunately, she's not at all alluring—something I honestly would have preferred.

FRIDAY, NOVEMBER 17TH

Night. Silence all around. I look out at the star-festooned heavens blanketing—no, smothering—the *colich*. It must surely be cool outside, but in here it's warm, protected. It was fine, I tell myself, everything went fine, but my voice doesn't sound like my own. I successfully weathered the first week but I'm still uneasy: something about this place escapes me. As I'm turning it over in my mind, my sister calls.

I had completely forgotten about her.

"What happened?" she asks. "Why haven't you called? I didn't even know if you got there okay."

Her voice is a rebuke.

"Of course I got here okay," I say. "Why wouldn't I have? And you'd know if something happened to me. It's not like the *guardia civil* would pay for my funeral if I had an accident."

She isn't amused, but she is persistent. She keeps complaining. She was worried, she says. She calls me inconsiderate, selfish. But her desire for details gets the best of her. She asks me what the *colich* is like, what documentation they asked me for, if I started teaching right away, how I'm getting on.

Too many questions at once.

I answer them in order, methodically: the school is peaceful and lovely; I've been teaching for five days; I'm doing the best I can; luckily no one has noticed anything, for the time being. I don't conceal the difficulty of those first days, my disorientation, the issue with the bathroom, the perpetual, devastating feeling of clumsiness and inadequacy every time I face the students.

"Well, I can't understand why," she says. "You wanted to be a writer, after all. There's not much difference between writing and teaching language."

"Oh, no? Is that what you think? They have nothing to do with each other. The greatest writers weren't school teachers."

"But you aren't a great writer."

An unimpeachable argument. I don't know what to say. She goes on:

"One would assume you know something about words. And you have to teach others how to use them. I don't see the problem."

No, maybe there is no problem. I feel brushed off.

"Careful now," I warn her. "This scheme of ours won't last for long if they've tapped the phones."

"Are you serious? Do you think they would do that?"

She sounds cautious, but still I detect a hint of dismissiveness. I know my sister well.

"Of course I do. This is a ritzy school. There are kids here whose parents are government ministers, big businessmen, actors—members of the mob, even. I wouldn't doubt it."

"Do you think they'll look into your background? What if he finds out?"

He is her ex-husband, my ex-brother-in-law. *He* is the one who should be here, had he not left her without any explanation. It doesn't bother me to be a bit cruel:

"He's not going to find out, dear sister . . . and you better accept that. He's gone, he's gone far away, to another country, across the ocean, maybe. He was smarter, or quicker, than the rest of us. What, do you think he'll come back to collect his documents?"

I picture my sister on the other end of the line. Looking old, upset. No one is coming back for her, that much is clear, but what if I *am* found out? If Señor J. or the assistant headmaster were to unmask me at one of their cryptic meetings? What would be the consequences for me, for her?

"It's better for you not to call," I tell her. "I'll call you soon."

We agree that I'll call her on Sundays. She makes me swear not to forget. Don't worry, I say, yawning. I hang up and sit by the window, not sure what to do.

I'm annoyed by our conversation. My sister is too much like me not to grate on my nerves, no matter what she does. Whenever she talks or complains, argues for or against something, it's like looking in a mirror. The way she has of curling her lip, her hand gestures, how she leans back when she's been offended, and forward to attack: all of that is inherited. And shared.

It's now completely quiet. I can see two figures in the distance, out beyond the playing fields, running through the shadows like they're trying not to be seen, or are hunched against the wind. I can't tell who it is. I can make out the shape of the mastiff and hear her bark.

Again, I wonder what would happen to me.

I try to relax: at the end of the day, it's no more than a question of having a degree, a name. Of being born into a particular family, staying on the right path, checking all the boxes, signing on the line, repeating the mistakes you've been taught, regurgitating what's required where you need to, being patient. And here you are—your degree, sir. You may call yourself *x* and practice the profession indicated below. I call myself by another name and practice a different profession at this *colich*; I teach my classes, I dress like a teacher, I want a teacher's dignity, his flexible authority, his steady stride. I have my students, my classes. I'm called to meetings and have the right to speak and vote in them. I have a room that someone cleans every day, my rations of food, a garden beneath my window, a place in the school, a job. Incredible.

And fragile.

So incredible I can't help but sense just how fragile it is.

SATURDAY, NOVEMBER 18TH

Weekends here are strange. Slow and tedious. People disappear, or retreat. There's an unhealthy stillness, something crouching behind the silence. I'm flattened by inertia, this glacial slowing of the hours. Am I complaining? Do I dare complain?

Certainly not.

No one has forbidden me from taking my old SEAT León and getting out of here. Only the students are restricted as to when they can or cannot leave. We faculty have to cover our on-call duties, but otherwise have the administration's permission to take time on our days off.

But I don't plan on leaving at the moment. I wouldn't know where to go. And so here I remain, at this *colich.*

I succumb to boredom and manage to get through the compositions I have left to grade. I go slowly, but when I finish, I still have much of the day ahead of me. I watch TV for a while. Start a new book. Look out the window.

It started raining today. The leaves on the trees swirl capriciously in the wind, knotting together before pulling apart again. I spend a good deal of time watching them, but avoid trying to make sense of their movements.

I grab my umbrella and decide to take a walk hoping to come across a colleague, but it's hopeless: the place is deserted.

I stroll the tidy grounds, a thoughtful, well-planned combination of arbors, small green plazas, benches. A verdant lawn extends beyond the gardens, always mowed and smelling of fresh-cut grass. The mastiff is always running out there, demented. Something isn't right with that dog: some kind of nostalgia, some memory of wildness. I call her, but she doesn't trust me and runs away.

My umbrella blows inside out every few minutes, but I keep my balance, careful not to step on the soaking wet grass. My feet slosh anyway. I make for the library, quick as I can.

The door is open. A Persian cat sits squarely in the lobby, its eyes on me. The silence is unsettling; not thick, exactly, but *thickening,* as if I myself were becoming slower, or heavier. There's an abnormal quality to the shadows. A sickly, intemperate temperature.

I leave immediately.

I circle around the dormitory buildings, which are divided into two wings, like the whole *colich,* and get as far as the colorfully painted annex they built for the scholarship students. Opposite is another annex, more sober, where the workers' dorms are located. Set on the top of a high slope, the houses of Señor J. and the assistant headmaster loom in the distance: ceremonious, red bricks, and gabled roofs.

I think I've gone too far. I turn back.

I walk along the forest's edge, alongside the metal fence punctuated with security cameras. Night descends over pine trees and eucalyptus. Fragrant and sinister, the trees conceal large, ugly birds that hoot, cackle, shriek.

I know nothing about ornithology. I can't tell them apart.

But maybe the birds can distinguish me from the school's other inhabitants. Maybe I'm the one being watched.

With wet clothes and muddy shoes, I return to my room. It's been cleaned in my absence. Someone has picked up my dirty laundry and changed the sheets, too. It's disconcerting that I still can't put a face to the person who does these things. This notebook was left open on the table. Anyone could have read it.

It's my mistake. I should be more cautious.

SUNDAY, NOVEMBER 19TH

Night again.

Still raining.

It falls with violence, soaking the dirt paths, dripping from tree branches. Louder than one would expect water to be.

The wind has died down.

I watch the rain fall in sheets, continuous.

Sundays seem to never end at this school. All this time in my room—all this TV and all this solitude—is affecting the quality of my skin, and maybe my spirit.

The sky cleared in the evening, the clouds thinning enough to admit the last rays of sunlight.

I decided to get outside and stretch my legs.

The earth smelled damp. Strange ants with green wings had sprung up all over the place, endeavoring to crawl through the grass, hectically climb tree trunks.

I spread a handkerchief out on a bench and sat down with my book.

I concentrated on reading, even though I wasn't really following the story of the obsessive man who locked himself in a limestone quarry with his paralytic wife so he could finish a scientific treatise on auditory perception. What a novel, I thought. Torture, imprisonment, insanity, illness. And yet, I was struck by the notion that this was all somewhat familiar to me: an indeterminate, disquieting similarity I couldn't place.

That's when he appeared.

That he would approach me so quietly was already strange in and of itself: only his shadow gave him away, once he was standing right next to me. I looked up. It was Señor J., smiling and observing me, stroking his goatee.

The conversation started out mundane. He asked me why I was out in such awful weather. I explained more than was necessary:

"I've been shut up in my room all day. I even ate lunch in there, alone. I needed to get some air."

"You don't leave on the weekends, then?"

"No, I haven't yet. I've only been here a few days. And I don't have a wife or children, as you know."

"No family at all?"

"Well, my sister, but she lives far away."

I hesitated briefly at this point. Since I was usurping the role of my ex-brother-in-law, my sister would have to be my ex-wife.

Would marital problems among the Wybrany staff be frowned upon? Divorces happened everywhere, but would Wybrany accept it as commonplace, or oppose it in favor of building a different, more pleasant world? Señor J. looked at me askance.

Intimidated, I cleared my throat.

"I'm recently divorced, as you know."

He still didn't speak. Uncomfortable with silence, I felt obliged to continue.

"It isn't what I would have chosen . . . I'm not in favor of divorce as the default. These days, people will separate over the littlest things . . . they don't have the skills to cope. But sometimes, when love is gone, it's the only thing left to do. Fortunately," I sighed. "we don't have children."

This was all true. They hadn't had children, a fact they mutually blamed on each other. The disgrace of infertility, turning away before the taboo: that was their life, every day of their life. The truth is, they should have congratulated one another: to have kids in families like mine just means producing more unhappy people.

But Señor J. wasn't interested in anything I was telling him. He crushed the winged ants with his shoe and resumed his questioning:

"I saw you out by the perimeter fence yesterday. Peculiar rounds you were making, Bedragare. You looked like a caged animal. Where were you going?"

It sounded like an accusation. I laughed, astonished.

"Nowhere," I said, adding: "But I didn't see you, sir."

"Naturally, Bedragare. It was raining. Under those circumstances, I behaved normally and stayed indoors. I saw you from my window. I was home with my wife, who was visiting." He paused, arched his brow. "I haven't gotten divorced."

I didn't know where this was leading. Uncomfortable, I patted the bench, offering him a seat. If this conversation were to continue, we had better be on the same level. He declined to give up his position of dominance. I made as if to stand up and he stopped me. It was clear he wanted us to continue as we were: him looking down on me, and me looking up. I noticed him eying my book, my filthy shoes.

"How are your classes?" he asked.

A simple "fine" wasn't an option. Flustered by my own lies, I described my intentions, teaching plans I came up with on the spot. He watched me with an ironic smile the entire time I was speaking, sizing me up. When I finished, he patted my shoulder and walked away in silence, leaving me with my last words on my lips.

I watched him lumber away, his enormous feet leaving deep prints in the muck.

And when he passed by her, I saw the mastiff shy away.

I returned to my room. The conversation had left me unsettled.

All of my clothes for the week were on my bed, washed and ironed. On the floor, I could still see the last damp passes of the mop. I had stashed my notebook away carefully this time. At least I hadn't forgotten to be cautious.

MONDAY, NOVEMBER 20TH

It's true that I had wanted to be a writer, but I lacked talent and courage.

Several years ago, a few of my stories were published in a magazine. They ran alongside stories by other, well-known writers, and so I thought I was just like them. I bought all the copies I could and passed them out to my co-workers, explaining that this was a big deal. They took the magazine in their grease-stained hands, looked at me without comprehension, and congratulated me as if I had just won back what I'd paid for a scratch ticket. I was perfectly aware that they didn't understand: this fact was precisely what made me feel like even more of a genius. An endless, tempting future awaited. I was intoxicated with myself.

But afterward, I couldn't write anything new, nothing longer than two or three pages at a time. All my stories lacked both coherence and an ending. Scenes bunched together, the characters were mostly incapable of action, the plot lumbered toward a halting, senseless denouement.

I protected myself with indifference and avoided facing hardship and failure. I began to keep a diary because I didn't have to make anything up. A simple log, a methodical, factual record. If I see rain falling outside my window, that's what I write. The only decision I have to make is whether to be concise or to describe the rain in detail. I can note how it changes over time, how heavy it falls, who gets wet and who doesn't. Or, I can simply write: *it's raining*. That's it. I write about what happens to me, why I think it happens, how I feel about it, what people tell me, how I respond. If something doesn't interest me, I don't write about it. Or I write a summary, strip it of meaning. I never have the urge to make anything up or change my story. I wouldn't be capable. My creativity has dried up, or maybe I destroyed it. Who knows.

Crazy Lola knew this and she made fun of me for it. I didn't let her read my diaries, but I know she studied them in secret.

"Do you actually think your life is interesting?" she would mock.

No, no it wasn't. Hers, on the other hand, might have been. An unstable, out-of-control woman tearing through the world like a tropical storm, exuberant and destructive. Always between tears and laughter, always on the edge: she'd had her punk, mystic, vegan, and promiscuous phases, her try-to-have-a-baby-at-all-costs phase.

That's where we left things.

She accused me of being a coward, resistant to change, manipulative. A repugnant, dull person. To top it off, the day I left with my clothes stuffed in grocery store bags, she bitterly added:

"Piece of shit wannabe writer."

Well, that was something. A writer—wannabe or not, piece of shit or not—was better than nothing at all.

When I arrived at the *colich*, my sister suggested maybe here I would find the peace I needed to write my novels.

"*Novels*, plural?" I laughed.

But behind my question was real excitement: Could I try? Would I have the peace, the courage?

Clearly, I do not. In this notebook, I've only written things that have happened since my arrival. This is not a novel. My imagination is still dormant. I'm paralyzed by reality. But this place is certainly a relief from the chaos of Cárdenas. I only have to worry about keeping up the façade, not showing my fear of being discovered. It doesn't seem like much, but this keeps me in a state of constant tension.

I'm not sleeping well. The slightest thing sends me reeling.

After a week, the school should feel familiar, and yet everything is still strange.

It's their way of acting, all of them—the teachers and the students, the employees and the administration, even the mastiff and the Persian cat.

In their own way, each one of them points to me as an intruder.

TUESDAY, NOVEMBER 21ST

Lately, I've had the impression that the students regard me with more than the usual disdain. They wait for me in class with mocking, observant faces. Always polite, of course, always restrained, but they're judging me. And they find me wanting.

In the older group, one boy sits in the back. His name is Ignacio, and he's the one who disturbs me the most. Scrawny, gimpy, very smart, he seems to exert some sort of unshakeable authority over the others.

I have a feeling that he draws little caricatures of me, or does impressions. Sometimes, he just sits and stares, like he's trying to transmit some kind of message. I can't punish him for looking at me, but there is undeniable insolence there. The kids all laugh quietly when I address him, or when he addresses me. I haven't been able to determine why that is.

I assign them a new composition and try not to obsess. Maybe I'm wrong about them. Maybe I'm using them as a way to reflect my own flaws, attributing thoughts to them that—deep down—represent what I think of myself.

It can be hard to gauge whether someone disapproves of us. Whether they're suspicious. Whether we're being snubbed. I sense disrespect, but maybe it's simple curiosity, or boredom. What am I to them but another teacher, after all? A boring, unimaginative teacher. A teacher who clearly isn't going to last long.

The boys look up from their papers now and then, chew their pens in thought. They pass notes between them, pencils and erasers. A sound of little *dings*, accompanied always by stifled laughter. A constant putting of hands in pockets, a silent typing I pretend not to see.

During class, time slows down and expands in such a way that these details carry more weight. I check the clock every five minutes.

Ignacio is always the first to hand in his work. His compositions are long and well-written, unsettling, and cruel—a blunt violence is always present in his dreams, power struggles, hierarchies, submissions. He is deliberate and cold. I never dare to make any comments.

As a budding writer, he is undoubtedly better than me.

WEDNESDAY, NOVEMBER 22ND

I've started to converse with other teachers this week. I'm making an effort to see them as normal people, no more peculiar or inscrutable than I am. Nevertheless, our conversations are banal. We sit in the dining hall and discuss the students, the incessant rain. I laugh along without really knowing why. I try to fit in, interpret their codes. Sometimes I get the impression that certain topics require a secret language, oblique signals, winks or watchwords, but I quickly dismiss the thought. We must all seem strange, from the outside.

Even Marieta stopped me in the hallway to chat. Marieta who is always in her own world, a step above the rest of us.

I was leaving class, a pile of papers under my arm. She looked me in the eye at first, and then at an indeterminate point somewhere above my head. The students watched us. I thought I saw Héctor elbow Iván, or the other way around.

It was the first time she spoke to me alone. Unfortunately, she only inquired about the basics: how things were going, if I was getting on okay, if I had any trouble with my classes.

I feigned nonchalance, even daring to make a bad joke that I would now rather forget. At one point, I took a miscalculated step backward—I was planning to lean against the wall—and all the essays fell to the floor. Embarrassed, I bent to pick them up, apologizing all the while. When I stood, she was already gone.

She rattles me, Marieta. Her grace, her obsessive efficiency.

Vivacity and petulance coursing through her small frame. She smiles, and her smile has all the beauty of a mask.

Her lack of interest in me is abundantly clear.

THURSDAY, NOVEMBER 23RD

I spend the most time with Martínez. Yesterday, I had lunch with him and we wound up in his room, playing chess.

Martínez is good-natured but competitive; he likes to win and can't help beating me quickly. The matches only last a few minutes: just enough time to show off his arsenal of express checkmates.

His room is bigger than mine, and his windows look out on the other side of the grounds. It's brighter. Neater and more comfortable.

He explains that he's worked at the *colich* from its earliest days, hence the privilege of a better room. He also tells me he's a widower, that his children live far away—which is fortunate, he adds—and that his life at Wybrany is the best thing he's got.

When he speaks, his eyes are so shrewd that I'm left doubting everything: his widower status, his children, even his thoughts on the *colich*.

Otherwise, he seems like a relaxed, canny old guy, a promising pal.

He tells racy jokes, goes on about *fútbol* and politics, doesn't hide his Andalusian accent. He seems like a different man from the one I've seen at meetings. He even goes so far as to poke fun at the assistant headmaster, whom he refers to as "Softy." He explains that Softy used to be the *colich* guidance counselor. That in other times, he was called the Advisor.

"Nice little nickname, eh? The Advisor. Softy was always trying to climb the ladder. He angled hard for that promotion."

He also has words for Señor J. According to Martínez, Señor J. is the *colich*'s principle investor. In the past, he's held political office, run a credit union, directed a foundation or two. He currently controls several lobbies.

"He isn't just anybody," Martínez assures me. "There are people very high up who back him, who are prepared to do what it takes to keep him happy. Same goes for the school counselor. They all come from high places."

The school counselor?

"Marieta? Marieta is powerful?"

He laughs at my surprise.

"Marieta's had a meteoric rise. She started at the *colich* as a young teacher three years ago and now look where she is. That's no coincidence—she comes from the Oscheffen. So if you're interested, Bedragare, forget it. She's not the girl for you. She's already occupied."

The Oscheffen? What the hell are the Oscheffen? A family of German aristocrats? A multinational appliance manufacturer? And what does he mean by Marieta being "occupied"? Occupied by what, by whom?

I want to ask him all of this but feel I shouldn't press. It seems more discreet to ask about my predecessor. What does Martínez know about him? Why was he on leave? Was he expected to return soon, or be out for a while?

"No one's told me anything," I say.

Martínez waves his hand, holding a bishop about to destroy my queen.

"Don't worry about it, Bedragare. Live in the moment, don't ask questions. None of the things tormenting you are the least bit important."

He obviously doesn't want to discuss the topic, either. He wins in a checkmate and immediately resets the board with a wink.

"Another game?"

He's insatiable, that Martínez.

FRIDAY, NOVEMBER 24TH

I'll admit it: sometimes even I forget what I did to get here. Only sometimes, but on those occasions I'm able to relax, as if I were convalescing after a long illness: good food, comfortable room, a reasonable, well-paid job, nice colleagues.

And yet, I could be discovered at any point. I'm hanging on by a thread, and my conscience punishes me. Betrays me.

And sometimes, reality knocks me over the head.

Like today. I almost gave myself away in front of Sacra. I can't stop replaying it.

The assistant headmaster had called a meeting and I ran into her on the way. Sacra, as I've said, is fat and meddlesome, but she doesn't seem a bad sort. Too fleshy, blunt, but friendly, fond of gossip, up for a chat, ready with a host of impertinent questions that—coming from her—somehow manage to sound completely natural.

"Where did you work before coming here?" she asks.

I had gone over the correct answer so many times that I unleash it too quickly. So quickly that she's surprised. Her brow furrows.

"When did you say you were at Vanter College?"

"When . . ."

I pretend to try to remember, but really I'm buying time. I start to get anxious and she seems to notice.

"Eight, nine years ago."

"But I was there then."

I correct myself:

"It may have been longer than that. I don't really recall, I've taught at so many places."

She insists, dogged and smiling.

"I worked there for twelve years. I would have seen you either way."

Luckily, we are already at the door to the assistant headmaster's office. We drop the subject, but the look she gives me suggests she won't easily forget.

"The thing is, your name is familiar, Bedragare," she whispers as we take our seats. "I recognized it the first time I heard it."

What a goddamn coincidence. Could this Sacra and my sister's ex really have been colleagues at some boarding school years ago? If so, this woman will figure me out, I'm sure of it. She'll have me by the balls.

But she doesn't say anything else, not a word. She just gives me another insinuating glance. An insinuation worse than any statement of fact.

The meeting starts and the assistant headmaster narrows his eyes, examining me. I pull out my papers, cross my leg over my knee. I don't know where to put my hands. I avert my eyes toward the Persian cat curled up in an armchair, apparently uninterested in moving any time soon.

No one dares shoo him off.

That cat has some kind of value, unquestionable and sacrosanct.

SATURDAY, NOVEMBER 25TH

This weekend is the last one of the month and the students have gone with their parents. The scholarship students stayed behind, of course. Their parents are always here anyway.

I've been bored stiff the whole day.

I correct compositions, watch TV, take a long nap, and walk the grounds, wondering if Señor J. is watching me from his window. For the first time, the mastiff allows me to pet her; a big accomplishment for me.

Martínez suggests a game of chess.

I'm not really in the mood, but I accept just for something to do.

We play in the teachers' lounge, which is almost always empty. There is a solid wooden table, upholstered chairs, a leather sofa marred by cat scratches, heavy drapes with metal holdbacks—all shrouded in the dusty, moth-eaten aura of unused spaces, no matter how often they're cleaned.

All the old cast-off pieces of furniture wind up there.

We drink whiskey and play game after game, a bunch of times in an hour, ten or twelve matches. I get drunk right away. I've never been a good drinker.

Martínez, on the other hand, is entirely composed. Red-faced but steady. He tells me he doesn't know what he'd do without his whiskey. The only time he leaves the *colich* is to go for provisions. He confesses that he never has enough. The wine served at meals is terrible, he says, early grapes, acidic, intolerable wateriness. I don't think it's that bad, but I hold my tongue because Martínez has a way of speaking about everything with authority. He squints, as if trying to recollect something.

"We did used to have good wine here, in the early days. But this place has gone downhill and the wine has only gotten worse. It's always the same."

I don't respond, but he must sense my doubt.

"This *colich* isn't even close to what it once was. They keep up appearances, yes, but I assure you: the truly powerful do not send their children here. Do you think they would let them mix with workers' kids? Share a room and eat sticky pasta three times a week? Pretense, appearances, a lot of *inglés* and very little excellence . . . that's all you'll find here. Not even the teachers are anything special . . ." He checkmates me.

Perhaps Martínez is right. I hadn't stopped to think about it. He clearly expects a reply, an argument. *What do you mean the teachers aren't anything special? I am,* I should protest. I should talk about my qualifications, my degrees, I should keep pretending just in case. Too drunk for that, I can only listen.

He goes on, claiming that Wybrany prefers to hire second-rate staff: dependent, unbalanced, imperfect. Those are the adjectives he uses. Martínez is as relentless a speaker as he is a chess player and whiskey drinker. He wipes his mouth on his sleeve and expounds on his idea: Wybrany would never recruit educators who were well qualified or prestigious. Too expensive. Too compromising.

"Before you were hired, did they give you any sort of test, Bedragare?"

No, of course they didn't give me any sort of test. No test at all. My sister's ex had filled out an application when the *colich* first opened. His name was on the list of substitutes. That was all. I suppose they simply reviewed the documentation I submitted. Nothing more. Now that I thought about it, it did seem strange.

"Here, the classes and who teaches them are the least of their concerns. What matters is the sense that one belongs in the upper echelon. Whether that's true or not is another question: the sense of belonging is what matters. And the teachers, clearly, do not belong at the top," Martínez takes a drink and shakes his head.

The sun sets. Seeing double, I walk through the gloom of the hallway to my room. Though my vision is blurry, I make out a figure at my door, hurrying to leave at my approach. She is slightly hunched, plump, her face wide and dark-skinned. She has big teeth and her eyes are enormous.

I'd swear it's the same woman who met me at the gate the day I arrived. I'm sure I've seen her elsewhere, cleaning or serving meals, but I never paid attention to her until now.

"Excuse me," she says, moving to step around me.

I try to stop her.

"Wait."

I'm not sure what to do next. I want to apologize for the cups of urine that first day, but I can't string the right words together. She looks up at me with a patient, bovine expression that actually kind of suits her.

I decide not to mention them, and just ask her name.

"Gabriela," she says.

"Do you always clean my room?"

"Always, sir. Before you arrived, too."

"Then you know the other teacher, the one I'm subbing for."

"Yes, sir. García Medrano, sir. I know he got sick."

I want to ask her to stop calling me *sir*, to stop addressing me so formally, but don't know how without being condescending.

"What did he have?"

I feel like I'm on the verge of getting the truth, or some valuable information at the very least. But Gabriela doesn't reveal much.

"That I don't know, sir, but I do hope he gets better soon. He was a good man."

I notice that she talks about him as if he were already dead. Her expression is serious and I would even say she seems to be directly affected by the situation. She's pensive, and adds:

"But it's also good that you're here now, sir. Everything has its positive side."

"Perhaps you're right," I say, and we stand in awkward silence.

I want to keep her there a little longer.

"Do you have children here?"

She answers quickly, firmly.

"I did, yes. A daughter, sir. Valentina. She left two years ago. She lives in Cárdenas now."

I tell her that I would have liked to have met Valentina, that I would have liked for her to have been my student, but it rings false and she can tell.

I let her go.

SUNDAY, NOVEMBER 26TH

I had an erotic dream about Gabriela. I woke up wet and confused.

Why Gabriela? She isn't attractive, at least not to my taste.

Is it because she makes my bed, scrubs my toilet? The eroticism of power, which I've never experienced before now?

I can't control my dreams. I shouldn't feel guilty, but I do. Outside the window, everything looks hazier than usual. Am I losing my vision? Isn't blindness a divine punishment?

My students haven't written about any erotic dreams in their compositions. Except that little flirt Irene, who continues to make veiled suggestions: "*We were sharing an ice cream. You held the cone and I licked the scoop . . .*"

I have a long day ahead of me and I can't shake this feeling. I'll go look for Martínez, see if he can distract me.

(. . .)

Sunday is over, thank god. Monotonous, too solitary. I didn't see anyone in the dining hall. I couldn't find Martínez, either. Maybe he went out for whiskey, or maybe he simply didn't want to answer the door when I knocked.

Obviously, I didn't insist.

The hallways were deserted. The *colich* seemed more isolated than usual. I heard some far-off cries, a shout of desperation that vanished in the air after several seconds.

I went back to my room and called my sister. I wasn't in the mood to listen to her, but I had to keep my promise. She must have been waiting for my call; she picked up on the first ring.

She's upset, she tells me everything in a rush. The city is ready to blow, she says. Gangs of rabble-rousers control the streets. It's very dangerous. It makes sense, I say. People are fed up, raising hell is the only way they have to protest.

"Fed up?" she says. "I'm fed up with so much robbery, so much broken glass, so much shouting, the police patrols, the assaults, the rock-throwing, the impunity."

This conversation bores me. It's always the same: complaint after complaint after complaint, laments piling up amid the most absolute indolence. I tell her my first month's salary will be in her account soon.

She perks up: money is always an excellent reason to face reality.

As we talk, I look out the window at the grounds, the impressive lecture hall covered in ivy, the playing fields surrounded by security fences. I think I see the assistant headmaster in the distance, holding something in his arms. Probably that hateful Persian. He walks toward his house at a fast clip. I watch as he grows smaller and disappears.

It's evening. The nice cars begin to arrive at the gate. The children are back. Beams from headlights crisscross the courtyard and gravel crunches under tires. The parents don't get out of their cars: it's late, and it isn't necessary. I imagine them kissing their children, hugging them inside their Mercedes, their Porsches, their Volkswagens, repeating the monthly speech by rote: take care of yourself, study hard, call me sometime, eat well.

The boys and girls step out of the cars, gym bags on their shoulders, an air of weary satisfaction. They hurry down the path, driven by the cold, calling to one another. The boys slap each other on the back, the girls give kisses. Back in their uniforms, hale and hearty.

Their figures are blurry, clouded by the distance, but I can almost make out their profiles. Ignacio's limp, the Goon's bulk. Beautiful Berta, swinging her hips.

My sister hung up a while ago. I stand with the phone pressed to my ear until I feel a chill—a chill deep in my bones—and I sit down to write.

Gabriela didn't clean today.

MONDAY, NOVEMBER 27TH

I made the bed and left my room neater than usual before leaving this morning. When I met her, Gabriela looked exhausted. There are lots of little doors like mine, and each one opens to a room that needs to be cleaned.

Besides, I still have that strange guilty feeling.

And I see Gabriela everywhere now.

Not Gabriela, exactly, but her kind.

Shy, dark faces that whisper among themselves but never interrupt us. Figures that are both almost invisible and constantly present: in the dining hall, on the grounds, up and down the hallways of the lecture building with their mops, pink uniforms buttoned to the neck.

There are men, too. Señor J.'s chauffeur, the security guards, the maintenance man, the porter. All dressed in blue or black with a servile, puppyish expression.

Like a god with his creations, I feel compelled to give each one a name.

I ask Martínez at breakfast and he points them out to me.

"That's Gabi. That's Tato. And that woman over there is Merche."

He stops and laughs.

"What the hell is going on with you? You don't even know the names of your students and you want to know about these people?"

"I met the one of the cleaning ladies. She looked worn out."

"Bedragare," he says. "They're very lucky to be here. Don't forget it."

"Yes, I suppose that's true."

"Their kids are here, too. You know that, right?"

"Oh, yes, the assistant headmaster told me at the first meeting. They repeat it every chance they get."

"So, what's the problem?"

Problem? I don't see any problem. Martínez has it wrong. It's my simple recognition of members of the same species, that's all. And the guilt I feel when Gabriela calls me "sir" and then I rail her in my dreams. Nothing that Martínez is likely to understand. I'm certainly not one to deny that they're privileged to work here, safe from the chaos outside. Like me. Like Martínez himself.

I look at him. "When it comes down to it, you and I are lucky, too, aren't we?"

He pats me on the back.

"Lucky? You think so?"

Stuffing himself with rolls and jam, he gives me his view of things:

"We are fortunate, Bedragare. The more mediocre one is, the deeper the hole he finds himself in, the more grateful he'll be when he's rescued. Our natural destiny would be miserable. And yet, here we are, enjoying breakfast in a top-notch institution."

He laughs as he speaks. I'm not sure how to respond.

"Are you being ironic, Martínez?" I ask after a moment.

"Look, Bedragare. I'll tell you something that'll make you reconsider your idea of irony." He takes a breath. "Would you believe me if I told you that the very last thing in the world I want is to retire? Retire? What for? What do I have to go back to? I've spent decades of my life here. Ever since my wife died. What would I do without Anita? In a world I no longer recognize as my own? I don't know what it's like outside, but I do know it's changed too much. I'm not prepared to adapt; I don't have the strength. Everything is simpler for me here. When I'm called to a meeting, I go, pretend to be serious, shuffle papers. That's all they require of me. Don't you realize? What do you think I'd have to do to make it on the outside? Can you even imagine? Am I young enough, strong enough for that? Do I have the wherewithal?"

Martínez has stopped eating. He's been looking in the distance as he speaks, his eyes narrowed, a grimace of disgust dancing on his lips. He turns to face me.

"So tell me, where's the irony in that? This *colich* is the best thing that's happened to me. You're lucky to be here, too. Believe me. Irony? Good Lord . . . can't you get this into your head?"

I'm dumbfounded. No doubt about it, Martínez dumbfounds me.

WEDNESDAY, NOVEMBER 29TH

Bad day today, bad day.

I had trouble with Ignacio in third period. I've never been in such a situation and wasn't sure how to respond. So I improvised. Disgracefully, it seems. I'm now convinced I'm a laughingstock.

It all started when a student—a shy, scattered boy—got up in the middle of class and tearfully approached my desk. The other boys carried on with their compositions without a peep. He stood before me, dripping snot, hiccupping, reluctant to speak.

I confess I felt more discomfort than pity. This student, one of the scholarship kids, is physically quite repulsive: greasy skin, reedy voice, the straight, limp, adolescent mustache of someone who's never shaved. In short, the kind of person I prefer to keep at arm's length whenever possible.

He faltered, but finally whispered that Ignacio was harassing him.

In the back row, Ignacio was diligently writing on his sheet of paper.

"How is he harassing you?" I asked.

He won't come out with it. In his sweaty hands, he holds a crumpled paper with writing on it.

"Give that to me," I said.

Suck my dick after class, you little bitch.

That's what it said.

I didn't know how to react. The boy was somewhat calmer. He watched me hesitate.

I walked through a sea of whispers back to Ignacio's desk. I showed him the paper. Ignacio read it carefully.

"It wasn't me," he said at last. "That's not my handwriting. Look."

I compared it to the writing on his paper and confirmed he was right: the handwriting was different. I considered this, probably longer than was necessary. The boy started to cry again at the front of the room. The others sniggered. I was compelled to take swift action.

"It isn't Ignacio's handwriting."

"He wrote that himself and now he's trying to blame me. Look, sir," Ignacio rushed to add.

He hands me the scholarship student's notebook. It was true: the same spotty ink, big dots over the *i*, round, childish letters.

I searched for an explanation. Forgery, I concluded.

"It's not hard to fake somebody's handwriting, Ignacio," I said.

Ignacio jumped to his feet and stood staring at me, his face inches from my neck. I could practically hear a growl rising from his insides. The class went silent, expectant. The boy at the front of the room had stopped crying.

"Get out," I said. "Get out of this class."

The boys looked shocked, all of them. What? Was it not acceptable to kick out a disobedient student?

Ignacio didn't move.

I persisted in spite of my doubts, repeating the order several times. I told him to go talk the assistant headmaster immediately. He would take my side, I was sure. I would tell him everything.

Ignacio slowly left the classroom, casting a grim, intimidating look over his shoulder. Every one of his movements was a threat.

I was shaken. Impossible to finish class normally, now.

The boys turned in their assignments, which were more poorly written than usual: lines crossed out, the edges of the pages creased. They hadn't even bothered to finish them. Surely they had sensed my qualms, my doubts.

Ignacio didn't return during the whole period.

(. . .)

The assistant headmaster was waiting for me in the dining hall. He motioned for me to sit beside him. His tone was one of affectionate concern, but he wore a clear look of disapproval. He chewed anxiously, eager to lecture me. I avoided looking at him when he spoke.

"I didn't know what to do," I argued. "The kids are usually so well-behaved. This incident completely caught me off guard."

He observed me, his fork suspended in the air.

"Ignacio didn't do anything."

"What do you mean he didn't?"

"He assured me that he didn't do anything. That boy tried to pin the blame on him for no reason. Schoolboy feuds; nothing serious. You needn't have made such a scene."

"Such a scene?"

"Throwing a student out of class! My God, when has this happened at Wybrany? Don't try telling me that they do it in public schools, that's no excuse. Or to be more precise, that's exactly why we *don't* do it here."

I was perplexed. I swallowed.

"So he won't be punished?"

"Who won't be punished? We're not in favor of punishment here. We prefer to educate, teach respect for rules. We mediate conflicts. We must find out what's going on between those two, talk to them. The students are splendid children; this will soon be sorted out, don't you worry. No one is sucking anybody off around here, you can be sure of that."

I blush.

"But," I say. "Ignacio isn't going to respect me."

"Why wouldn't he? Ignacio is a good boy. He has his quirks, that's all. He had problems when he was young and his self-esteem is low because of his limp. His parents tended to be overprotective, which has resulted in certain . . . interpersonal difficulties. But he's a splendid boy, I assure you."

Then he glanced around and, lowering his voice, mentioned Señor J.

"He's always been very close to the boy. Ignacio is a kind of personal wager, a challenge. Ignacio was so very . . . weak, in the beginning. You wouldn't have recognized him. I *will* say that, from my point of view, he is excessively sheltered. But the headmaster must know what he's doing, and why. I don't involve myself in his personal affairs."

This allusion was disconcerting. What are you saying, I wanted to ask, but the question stuck in my throat. Softy stopped looking at me and returned to his meal.

We ate in silence. I noticed the other teachers watching us. Maybe they knew what had happened and were talking about it, judging me. I thought I saw Sacra gave me a wink. Ledesma avoided my eye.

Before he stood, the assistant headmaster gave me a parting piece of advice:

"Ask for help when you need it, Bedragare. You still have a lot to learn."

Naturally I have a lot to learn. I still don't understand what I'm expected to do when two students fight, especially if one is a scholarship student. I don't understand why certain students are afforded special protections that also serve the protector, nor the innuendos everyone sows about everyone else. The truth is, as time goes on, I understand less and less.

(. . .)

I run into Gabriela in the hallway on my way back to my room. She's hunched over the mop, enveloped in the funk of bleach and floor polish. Sweat beads on her forehead. Even though she looks exhausted, I want to tell her what happened. I need to get it out.

"You know, sir, this kind of thing happens in schools all the time. I'm surprised that you're shocked. You must've seen it before."

I bluff.

"Oh, sure. I'm sure I've seen it before. But how can I put this? I didn't expect it at this sort of *colich*, Gabriela. Everything is so regulated, so disciplined. The words on that note . . ."

She looks up at me with bloodshot eyes.

"Bad things happen everywhere. You ought to know, sir."

Then she moves away in silence, her wearied body vanishing in the shadows.

THURSDAY, NOVEMBER 30TH

I had a terrible dream last night. I dreamt I was going blind. Crushed by darkness, surrounded by ravenous shadows, I stretched my hands out into the void.

I woke up, heart racing, blinking in the pitch black. I felt around for the light switch and checked the clock: it was only 5 A.M. I thought I had lost my vision, that I was losing it by the minute. I spent two agonizing hours opening and closing my eyes, diagnosing myself until I finally fell asleep again. When the alarm went off, I didn't hear it.

Late for class.

As I ran down the hallway, I had the sensation that everything was blurrier, less defined. I lost my sense of clarity a long time ago. The world seems like a work of fiction; the things that happen are like projections on a movie screen. They flicker before me and I have nothing to do with them. I can't change—or even understand—them.

They happen right before my eyes, nothing more.

(. . .)

Ignacio is leaning calmly against the classroom doorway, as if nothing out of the ordinary had occurred the day before. When he walks by me on the way to his seat, he stares and slows his step. The students are all transfixed by this scene, all except for the boy on scholarship. He sits in the corner, completely motionless.

The air is charged with expectation. The boys sit, their heads cocked, feeling me out, interrogating me in silence. I don't know what to tell them.

Later, Marieta approaches me at the entrance to the dining hall.

She looks like she has something urgent to say. Blinking nervously, she blurts out:

"I have to speak with you. We need to meet."

An ultimatum. I suppose she wants to talk about what happened yesterday, or rebuke me for arriving late to my classes. I search her eyes. Metallic gray, cold and distant.

I ask why.

"To discuss your pedagogical methods."

My methods? What methods? I don't follow any method, except that of survival. I don't say that, obviously. In fact, I lead her to believe that I'm very much interested in hearing her advice.

"It's come to my attention that you take a rather . . . *peculiar* approach to your classes," she explains. "Perhaps you need a bit of guidance. Remember, Wybrany parents are demanding. You have to offer high quality, innovative instruction. That's what is expected of us at Wybrany. You can never be too careful."

She's pretty when she talks like this. The slighty jutting upper lip, the straight little white teeth. I fake interest, nod my head, I'm all ears.

She checks her planner, flips through the pages with a commanding index finger. We can meet on Monday, she says, next Monday at five.

Plenty of time, but I don't have a clue how to prepare myself.

Deepening unease, that's the sense this appointment gives me.

SATURDAY, DECEMBER 2ND

Another weekend at the *colich*. I spend a lot of time in front of the window. The wind sweeps over the lawn, a trash can rolls away downhill. Storm clouds build in the distance. We've hardly seen the sun in days.

This week of classes wore me out. My free time in the afternoon doesn't compensate for the stress of every morning, the continual shifting between pretense and mockery, appearance and uncertainty.

The boys make fun of me, there's not a doubt in my mind.

And led by Irene, the girls do too.

They seemed so well behaved in the beginning, such *splendid* kids. Sure, you would glimpse a hint of suspicion or snideness now and then, nothing consequential. It all seemed so simple. I read what I wrote before: *I've realized that being a teacher is easy, in the end. You walk into class, decide what they have to do, and then they do it.*

I tried to believe in those words, to convince myself that my own feelings of guilt have led me to imagine their mistrust. But it isn't true.

Things are happening around me that I can't grasp. My head is ready to burst, overflow.

Maybe I'm getting sick.

I remember Gabriela's "bad things," which apparently do happen everywhere.

(. . .)

I stop by the teachers' lounge in the afternoon to see if Martínez is around.

I find the room unusually animated. Half a dozen teachers are playing cards. Martínez plays with them. Barely glancing up when he sees me, he hollers a greeting:

"Welcome, Bedragare! Join us!"

On one side, Ledesma is shuffling his cards listlessly. Hernández and Prieto—two teachers who look like twins and go everywhere together—are also in attendance, along with fat Sacra and a woman named Consu, the scholarship students' tutor.

I settle in at the table.

Martínez is euphoric, almost unbearably so. He pats everyone on the thigh, even the women, with a familiarity that seems out of place. He drinks whiskey from a silver flask and wipes his mouth on his sleeve.

We play several hands. He wins every time, but Sacra's not far behind. Excessive and enthusiastic, she shouts and jumps up with every hand. I can see she makes Ledesma uncomfortable.

Lux observes us intently from the couch in the corner.

Martínez finishes his whiskey, stands, and heads toward me, a look of delight on his ruddy face.

"Now Bedragare will battle me in a chess duel. I'll get the board and a little something to celebrate with," he winks, shaking the flask.

He leaves with a slam of the door. I'm not in the mood to play along.

I sit down with Ledesma, who strokes his mustache, distracted.

Ledesma is a good-looking guy, with a sad, oblivious air and the moody expressiveness of his thick eyebrows. He interests me all of a sudden.

I give him a wink.

"Martínez is in rare form today."

"Yes," he says.

That's all.

I smile, unsure what to say next. I can see Sacra watching me, blinking. Lux stretches himself awake, arching his back. Silence. I suddenly feel hot, a warmth dragging me into apathy and stupor. What am I doing here? Maybe the world is coming apart and I've yet to notice.

I decide to leave before Martínez gets back.

Ledesma catches up to me outside.

"Do you mind if I join you a minute?" he asks.

Of course not, I smile. The request is unexpected, and welcome. Together we walk to the edge of the woods.

Ledesma is an odd character. He hangs on the metal fence and stares at the horizon in silence. All my attempts at conversation fail.

All except one. I ask him about García Medrano and his reaction is surprising.

"Did I know him? Of course I knew him!"

Wind swirls around us. The mastiff comes and licks my hand. All at once it's too cinematic. Something is obviously going on here.

"What was he sick with? Why is he on leave?"

"Oh, nobody knows. Didn't the assistant headmaster tell you?"

"The assistant headmaster? No, he hasn't told me a thing. He's always very pleasant, too pleasant, but honestly, I don't think he approves of me," I admit.

"Don't worry, he doesn't approve of anyone."

"Señor J. didn't tell me anything, either. I thought those two were thick as thieves, but I've begun to notice some differences in opinion. The assistant headmaster made some strange insinuations about Señor J. that I'm not sure I understood correctly."

"Señor J. and the assistant headmaster can't stand each other. I'm glad you figured it out so quickly. With regard to the insinuations, they all could make them. Plenty of matters that are best kept secret. The thing is to pretend you don't notice."

"I don't know, Ledesma. It hasn't been easy, figuring these things out."

Ledesma lifts his gloomy eyes to the sky.

"The assistant headmaster is in his position because of his connections. He even got rid of the previous assistant headmistress, a woman who had been here since the founding of the *colich*."

"And Señor J. allowed that? I assume he's equally powerful . . ."

I think of what Martínez said about his stocks, his lobbies, his political positions.

"Yes, he's very powerful. But he's also lazy. Sometimes, two powers are needed to balance each other. Those two in particular maintain a certain equilibrium, based in transactions."

My head feels warm.

"Transactions? What kinds of transactions?"

He arches his brow.

I'm tired of everyone speaking in code all the time. The mastiff is still going in circles around us, just like our stalled conversation. It's cold and I'm starting to feel dizzy.

"Look, Ledesma, if you know something and want to tell me, great. And if you don't know anything or don't want to tell me, that's also fine. But don't treat me like an idiot."

He lowers his eyes and says quietly:

"I don't know any more than what I've told you. I'm sorry."

I make a conciliatory gesture. At the end of the day, I prefer his reticence to Martínez's excess.

We head back. A group of boys is playing soccer on the lawn. *Splendid* boys overcoming the adverse weather conditions, as Softy would say.

I just want to go to bed.

Ledesma stops at the entrance to the building and looks at me closely.

"Gabriela was the person who knew García Medrano best. I imagine you know who she is. One of the cleaning ladies. She'll be able to tell you more about what happened."

I see Martínez waiting for me impatiently, motioning on the other side of the window. He roars with raucous laughter, calls to us, holds up the chessboard to entice me.

I go inside and play two games just to shut him up. He beats me in two minutes, one per game.

SUNDAY, DECEMBER 3RD

I needed to see Gabriela but wasn't sure how to run into her casually.

She's elusive. She keeps to the shadows: she's become accustomed to being invisible, which is her escape.

I'd noticed that on the weekends she comes to clean my room as soon as I leave. How she is aware of my comings and goings, I don't know, but in order to draw her in, I set my trap like a spider and pretend to go out for a walk.

I put on my jacket and grab my umbrella. I turn down the path that runs through the arbor and out toward the playing fields. I walk a little farther, counting the minutes, and when I think I've given her enough time, I turn back.

I was dead on. As I open the door, I see her with her back to me, scrubbing the sink with a scouring pad.

"Oh, I'm sorry, sir. I thought you wouldn't be back for a while."

"No need to apologize," I say. "You're cleaning things I get dirty. I'm the one who should apologize."

She straightens, brushing her hair from her face.

"But this is my job, sir."

"Do you like your job?"

"Yes, I do, sir."

"Isn't it hard on you, cleaning all day?"

"No, sir. I don't know anything else. It was hard when I worked in the city. They didn't pay well. I didn't have a break. But here, it's different. There are lots of us and we take shifts. It isn't that much work."

"And your children are safe here."

She nods silently.

"You had your daughter here," I add. "Mixing with the *crème de la crème*, a valuable education at no cost. That's a good thing, isn't it?"

"Yes, sir. Our children are very well-off here."

She's toeing the official line. I search her eyes for acquiescence, or fear, but all I see is an astonishing emptiness, perhaps slight surprise at my questions.

I'm uncomfortable.

I decide to just come out with it and ask about García Medrano. All at once something changes. A startled look, an anxious smile.

"I already told you, sir, I don't know why he got sick."

"But you knew him well? You had contact with him?"

She purses her lips. A flash of what could be mistrust—however fleeting—passes over her face.

"I don't know what you're referring to, sir. What kind of contact?"

She obviously feels cornered, which wasn't my intention. Inadvertently, my question had seemed suggestive. Her discomfort supplied an answer different from the one I'd hoped to hear.

What sort of relationship had they had?

I calm her, assure her I wasn't referring to anything out of the ordinary. I had simply heard very good things about my predecessor and hoped she could help me find him, that was all. I haven't lost sight of the fact that I'm just his substitute. I want to do a good job, but I lack his experience at the *colich*. I have doubts when I'm teaching sometimes and wish I could consult his papers, even speak with him and ask for help. Being a teacher isn't as easy as it might look, I add.

Gabriela shrugs and nods toward my desk.

"But you have his teacher's notebook, sir."

She's right. I've had it since the first day, but there's nothing of interest in it, just the students' file cards and their grades. That slanted, hurried handwriting, simple everyday notations.

There had to be more. More facts. How long had García Medrano been working at the school? Did he leave on the weekends? Did he store his personal belongings at Wybrany? Did he take them with him when he left? Were they being held somewhere?

Gabriela shakes her head the whole time. She insists she knows nothing. She doesn't think he left the school very often, but she can't be sure. He was a normal teacher, normal behavior, polite, middle-age, discreet, and studious.

"He was like you, sir," she concludes.

Me, discreet and studious? I'm amused. I laugh softly and accept that the conversation has reached a dead end. Maybe it's enough to hear her use the past tense, *he was*. It seems finished. Obstructed, for sure. Gabriela looks impatient: the scouring pad is still in her hand, foam waiting to be rinsed accumulates in the sink. I thank her for her patience and leave so she can finish.

Poor Gabriela. I pressed her, took advantage of this insidious hierarchy.

It's Ledesma's fault. What was he hinting at? Where did it lead? What was he trying to do when he mentioned Gabriela? Confuse me, confuse her?

I go back out to the grounds and sit on a bench out of sight of Señor J.'s window. I wait.

A figure approaches from the distance, but I can't make it out with any certainty. Every time I get tense—which happens too often lately—sparks and stains float before my eyes. I get muddled. The figure draws near and something about it reminds me of Sacra—the obese body, generous bosom, that tilting, satisfied walk. I'm not sure it's her, but I flee anyway. There's no one I want to talk to.

Gabriela is gone by the time I get back to my room. Everything clean, everything tidy. I flop down on the bed, assaulted by an incomprehensible desire to cry.

(. . .)

I just remembered my sister. It's Sunday. I have to call her.

I have no interest in doing so, but I do.

A predictable conversation. She's still afraid. I try to reassure her, but she tells me I don't know what I'm talking about, that I'm not there to witness what is happening.

Shots were fired below her window the other night. The police used tear gas. She said she saw a man smashed against the door to the pizzeria, the pizza box destroyed at his feet, the food just pulp spilled on the sidewalk.

"You need to stay inside as much as possible," I tell her.

"But I have to look for work, do the shopping."

"Don't worry about work. I already told you, you can count on my paycheck every month. And do the shopping early in the morning. One person doesn't need much. Store up provisions, like ants do. Then don't go out again for the rest of the day."

I don't know if she understands me. It's like speaking to a small child. She fusses the whole time, sputters that she doesn't want to live like a captive, murmurs something else, unintelligible.

Then she asks me about the *colich*. She sighs with envy when I tell her about it. I sense that it's good for her to keep believing that this place exists exactly as she imagines it, and so I go on. I describe a refuge, idyllic and remote, an oasis of education and peace.

Since the sham is already well underway, I also tell her that I've started working on a novel.

What does it matter, in the end?

One more lie. I tell them all the time.

MONDAY, DECEMBER 4TH

I met with Marieta today. Her pretenses weren't false: in effect, she was concerned about what she called my "pedagogical methods." She cut right to the chase.

Why was I always assigning compositions? Is that all I did with the students? All I've done since I arrived at Wybrany?

I confess, but quickly mount a defense.

"I planned to dedicate this trimester to written expression. It's an important part of language learning."

"But why just the compositions? You could incorporate other activities."

"Writing these pieces is the best way to determine the students' abilities. The compositions are simply a road leading to something else in the future. I plan to do other things."

I know my lies don't sound credible. She looks at me coldly and I avert my eyes. Her spotless, organized office is dominated by metal and the color white. She neatly shuffles the papers in front of her, dressed in white as well, and wearing a silver necklace. When she addresses me, her voice is cool:

"A mother has complained that you oblige the students to write about their personal dreams. Dreams, Isidro, belong in the realm of intimacy. Don't you think?"

A mother complained? That's funny. Even funnier when I discover it was Irene's mother. Irene, my sweet student with the prominent jaw and lazy eye.

I don't go into detail with Marieta so as not to further complicate matters, but I'm circumspect. Of Irene, in particular.

"They weren't forced to tell me their real dreams. Lots of them made things up. The topic of dreams was just a pretense to get them writing. There's no mystery here."

"These children are more innocent than we think," she says. "If you order them to write their dreams, they're not going to make them up. Therein lies the problem, Isidro. Seen from the outside, it looks like you were trying to exercise some kind of psychological control over them."

Psychological control? Innocent children? She couldn't possibly be referring to my students. I feel like I've landed on a different planet.

"Moreover, compositions are an outdated teaching method," she adds. "They're hardly used anymore."

She talks to me about books, authors, theories, a smooth erudition that unfurls on its own accord. Her eyes remain calm; it's an unseeing look, one that grazes and burns at the same time.

She's determined, indomitable. I like dominant women, so I set aside my arguments and submerge myself in her voice. I don't want to ruin this encounter; at least she's made an effort to be cordial and in the end, I suppose, she's only doing her job.

I tell her she's right. Okay, I recognize that the compositions are a little anachronistic and that it's unusual to assign them every day. I can admit that. I pledge to use other methods. I apologize for making my students uncomfortable.

For a moment she looks alarmed. Did she think I was mocking her by giving in so easily? But she quickly relaxes and a satisfied expression spreads across her face. Mission accomplished.

The meeting ends and I leave without a shred of hope.

No, Marieta doesn't look at me the way I look at her.

TUESDAY, DECEMBER 5TH

Today, I say in class, you are going to write your last compositions. Or the last ones for a good long while, in any case. But don't worry: this time, I'm not going to ask you to write about your dreams. I don't want you to feel like your privacy has been violated.

I emphasize the word *privacy* and look at Irene, who returns my look impassively, lips pressed together. Her face remains unchanged when I propose the new topic:

"You are going to write a story about me, about how you could hurt me. Fiction allows for this kind of thing. Therapeutic violence, let's call it, nothing I'll hold over you later. A story about how you could ruin my life, that's all. Give free rein to your animosity. Be perverse. Have fun. Today, nothing is out of bounds."

I repeat the same speech in each one of my classes. All are left bewildered. Even Ignacio lifts his head and looks at me, surprised, a startled blink that could almost appear innocent.

They take turns asking questions, complaining, bickering.

"Are you sure you won't get mad?"

"I can't think of anything!"

"I'd rather tell you about last night's dream."

"Can we really write whatever we want?"

I tell them to quiet down. I address their doubts, the class settles. They write on their sheets of paper and I look out the window in the meanwhile. Everything is routine and peaceful. I still have that sense of images projected on a screen, a vague *déjà vu.*

I don't know what came over me, what led me perform this bit of audacity, but I suddenly feel more confident. Less afraid.

Later, the students set their papers on my desk. From the corner of my eye, I glance at some of the paragraphs.

Traditional version: We hired a hit man to kill you. He was huge, ripped, almost 200 kilos, used to torturing and killing mercilessly. When the fateful night arrived, he entered your room and found you deep asleep. He was ready to strangle you with his enormous hands, but up close you reminded him of his father, from whom he had been estranged since childhood. His eyes filled with tears and he couldn't kill you. But to prove he'd done it, he brought us a dog's eyes and tongue, assuring us they were yours . . .

Fantastical version: Just like in *Alice in Wonderland,* someone gave you a potion to drink that shrunk you and turned you into a little tiny creature. A student put you in a hamster ball and we played ping-pong with it . . .

Cowardly version—with spelling errors (a scholarship student, obviously): a groop of people wanted to beat you up, some of us tried to help you but we couldn't do anything, it was imposibble. They left you with a messed up face and a missing leg.

Vengeful version with Borgesian overtones: The Headmaster ordered you to write compositions not only about your dreams but about everything you saw around you: conversations you heard, things happening at Wybrany, things you saw and didn't see, the past and the future, too. You spent all day writing, but you never had enough time to write it all. You stopped eating. You couldn't let yourself miss a single minute. You became so thin that you wasted away, nothing but skin and bones . . .

Irene is the last student to turn in her assignment. I set aside her paper to look at it in my room.

I've just finished reading it.

The title is written in rounded, uppercase letters. Explicit: WHAT I WOULD DO TO RUIN YOUR LIFE. And then: *To ruin your life, I would put a pair of panties in your briefcase. I would take naked pictures of myself and put them between the pages of your books. Then I would tell my mother and we would report you. The evidence would be irresistible. They would give you life in prison . . .*

Disturbing girl, that Irene. Even though she confused *irresistible* and *irrefutable*. I mark it with a red pen and take a rest.

FRIDAY, DECEMBER 8TH

My new focus for the week: teaching methods.

After many trips to the library, I still can't manage this linguistic terminology.

How could it possibly be useful to fill kids' heads with all this conceptual baggage?

Language stripped of life, of flesh, gutted: that's what I think of syntactical analysis. Semantics: dead words under a magnifying glass, meaning in the throes of death like a fish flopping out of water. Phonetics: incomprehensible babble, harsh stutters.

What can I say? This subject is of absolutely no interest to me.

But it is useful for passing the time.

The library is housed in a room with long wooden cross-beams and a checkered tile floor, the geometric patterns made to look antique. Dark wooden shelves and tables with little lamps and computers are arranged neatly throughout the entire space: a blend of modernity and tradition that isn't at all appealing. A faint, greenish light illuminates the heads of the few students who have come here to study.

I'm assisted by an inexperienced young woman, completely lacking in charm: dyed blonde hair cut too short, bulging eyes, flat chest. I think she comes and goes from the *colich* daily, who knows from where. I don't care to find out, just as she doesn't care about my sudden interest in didactic texts. Stuffed into her suit, she speaks to me between yawns and has a visible distaste for anything other than the magazines hidden under her desk.

Silence and emptiness. Since becoming a regular, I've rarely come across any colleagues in the library. Just Ledesma, on one occasion. He raised his eyebrows in a hint of a greeting but otherwise didn't move—sunken shoulders, elbows on the table—as if he had completely forgotten our conversation at the edge of the woods. He is a peculiar one.

Hours and hours spent consulting books with instructions and answer keys. Hours and hours tangled up in the online data bank. All that material, still incomprehensible and useless.

SATURDAY, DECEMBER 9TH

While I was miles away in my own thoughts, Marieta approached me in the library.

She broke through my daydream, peering over my shoulder to see what I was reading. She seemed pleased. After the chilliness of Monday's meeting, her tone was somewhat friendlier: agile, transparent. She emanated something akin to happiness—limited, perhaps, excessively contained—but happiness nonetheless.

For some unknown reason, she suggested we get coffee. She was deigning to speak to me. I couldn't refuse.

Gabriela was helping in the kitchen that weekend, and waited on us. I felt a bit anxious: uneasy that Gabriela was seeing me with Marieta and worried that Marieta would pick up on my familiarity with Gabriela.

"Sir, miss," she said, setting the cups on the table.

Then she disappeared discreetly.

Marieta was radiant. The floor lamp bathed half her face in light, and her skin looked soft and warm. I wanted to touch her. I contemplated her at length, captivated. She looked at me intently, chatting away, though she was as restrained and discreet as always.

Whenever I'm with a beautiful woman, I have a suspicion that the universe has made a terrible mistake. I feel guilty or insecure or afraid that someone—someone merciless, unknown—will recognize the error and punish me. But nothing happened, at least nothing like that. Marieta was relaxed and even seemed inclined to confide in me.

"I haven't been feeling well lately," she said. "I'm not sleeping—I'm troubled by strange thoughts."

This was undoubtedly not true—she looked wonderful. Did she hope I would take up the subject, confess my own unease? I didn't—there was little I could do except smile stupidly.

As I watched her, I thought I glimpsed Señor J. through the window at her back. I squinted and she turned to look behind her.

"Oh, it's nothing," I said. "My eyes give me trouble sometimes. I was trying to see who it was."

Yes, she confirmed. It was Señor J. He was strolling around the grounds with his wife. A round young woman, very blonde. I recalled Señor J.'s comments about her, the woman he hadn't divorced *yet*.

I would have liked to ask Marieta about them, to find out more about Señor J. or the assistant headmaster, or even García Medrano, but I knew that was a wall I couldn't breach. Everything Marieta said with regard to the *colich* was steeped in praise. It would be useless to ask, and would probably just raise suspicion. I couldn't get her to talk about herself, either: did she receive visitors, too? Did she have someone outside the *colich*? Why had Martínez said she was "occupied"?

"Don't you ever leave on the weekends?"

"I can't, I just can't," she said. "My responsibilities here are too great. I can't afford to leave."

That was all. That, and few blinks of her evasive eyes. To be honest, she seemed more interested in asking questions than answering them.

"And you?" she said. "Don't you ever get out?"

"No, not at the moment . . ."

"But you get along with your colleagues, right? I've seen with you Martínez, especially."

"Oh, sure. Martínez is a good guy. We play chess, we talk . . . he's always in a great mood."

"And Ledesma?"

"What about Ledesma?"

Alarm bells.

"Ledesma isn't very happy," she said.

"No, he isn't." I hesitated. "But I don't know him well. We've barely spoken a handful of times."

"Ah, I thought I saw you together, out in the field."

Apparently, everyone knows what happens outside the walls of the *colich*. Were we under surveillance? I shook my head, dismissing the thought.

"We've had a few normal conversations. He's very quiet. We don't even have any students in common."

Marieta finished her coffee and looked at me with a smile, as if she were saying something more than what I understood. The conversation was over. I left a short while later with the uncomfortable feeling of having been duped. Our coffee date had simply been an excuse to take my psychological pulse, in the end. What had I expected? That she was actually interested in me?

I'm beginning to realize that every day here has an emasculating aftertaste.

SUNDAY, DECEMBER 10TH

A small group of us ate lunch together today. This is unusual for a weekend: those of us who have nowhere to go usually confine ourselves to our rooms, out of pride or embarrassment. But this time, Martínez was able to bring us together with his enthusiasm. We had been spread out among the tables and he managed to gather us together, making a big fuss, not even waiting for our consent. Did we want to sit together? It didn't matter.

We talked and laughed, conducted by Martínez's baton. I only participated indirectly. I watched Ledesma, who had isolated himself in a corner. His baleful eyes met no one else's, not even mine. He barely ate. His fork came and went, empty, from plate to mouth,

mouth to plate. He didn't seem conscious of what he was doing.

He was the first to get up and leave the dining hall, muttering an inaudible goodbye.

I was also tempted to leave but Martínez sat down, elbowing me in the ribs.

"I can't believe you're such a moron," he said. "Are you really going to pass up this chance?"

I had no idea what he was talking about.

"What chance?"

"You're blind, Bedragare. Sacra will do anything you want."

Sacra? I watched her, colossal and smiling, tucking into dessert. The suggestion was shocking. What did he mean? What did he know about Sacra? What were they up to? Had they been talking about me? Did they have some kind of relationship?

I answered him rudely.

"Why don't you screw her yourself?"

I immediately felt compelled to apologize, but he laughed and grabbed my arm.

"You think I haven't?"

Sacra looked over and stared at the both of us. In all likelihood, she had heard our conversation, but wasn't affected by either our obscenity or contempt. Her little friend Consu looked amused, as well. She was laughing, her mouth stained with whipped cream. Like a ridiculous child. This plotting was repulsive. Were they making fun of me?

I feigned indifference and stayed a bit longer at the table.

When I stood to leave, Sacra got up, too, and suggested we take a little stroll. I told her I was too tired for a walk.

She smiled and said loudly:

"*Ay*, Isidro. You're always blowing me off . . . even though we've been colleagues before. Didn't you tell them? Didn't you all know?"

She turned to them.

"Did you know that Isidro and I were at the same school a few years ago? A different *colich*. Vanter College, isn't that right, Isidro? Even though he seems so timid, such a newbie . . . he actually has a great resume."

She continued to smile, slyly watching me from the corner of her eye. She didn't even seem annoyed; she simply enjoyed backing me into a corner. I didn't know what to do. Argue? Explain? How best to stop her? I opted to keep silent.

I saw the others sitting there, watching us, understanding all of it. I returned to my room as soon as I could. I was dizzy. Sacra's words echoed in my head.

I had definitely drunk more than I should have.

(. . .)

But there was one surprise left. I hadn't been in bed ten minutes when someone knocked softly on my door. Two little taps, then silence. I opened warily. It was Gabriela. She wouldn't meet my eye. She carried a plastic bag under her arm.

She explained that they were García Medrano's papers.

"I brought them for you, sir. Maybe they'll help."

"But what are they? And why do you have them?"

She gestured vaguely. She seemed in a hurry. She said she was in a rush, she had to go. She had only brought them in case I wanted to take a look. They weren't important.

Confused, I thanked her and took the papers.

I stood watching as she made her way down the hall, the papers in my hand and my head still spinning from the booze. Had she been a vision? No, no: I was holding the papers of someone who was apparently a secret around here. Someone about whom it was better to keep quiet, at least. Tangible, legible papers. Perhaps I could write a novel about this, after all. A mystery novel. A thriller.

I went back inside and lay down to read. I had to reread the pages several times, and I don't think I can chalk up their incomprehensibility to being drunk.

Twelve pages total. It appears to be the outline for a story, or maybe an essay. A mix of typed and handwritten pages. The action, which is confusing, takes place in an imaginary city with a brutal, medieval way of life based on trading. Little girls locked in cells appear obsessively throughout the text. Heroes and mercenaries, too. The handwriting is tight, tense. Lots of words are crossed out, the paper stained with drips of coffee and olive oil.

I don't think I can decipher all this.

(. . .)

I call my sister that night. Everything is still the same: her nerves are frayed, the city is unraveling. The money is in her account, the joint account she shared with her ex and which she now manages alone, fortunately. There isn't much else to talk about. I want to get off the phone quickly; I tell her I'm exhausted. It isn't a lie. She's tired, too. We don't say much. Short, veiled sentences.

It could be that in times like this, communication is impossible.

MONDAY, DECEMBER 11TH

Things are going even worse for me, now that I've kicked off a new phase of classes that include syntactic analysis, literary chronologies, and other such nonsense. I'm more of an imposter than ever, in this profession which is not my own.

The students are inquisitive, they're interested, turning their minds to grammatical trifles, paying such close attention that I contradict myself, make mistakes.

I keep the answer keys under my desk, but it's no use: the class outwits me every time.

Ignacio appears to have risen from the ashes. He decides which flank to attack from and asks me precisely what I don't know. He watches very carefully as I answer and doesn't say a single word. His look throws me off balance. I stutter, stumble over my words. The boys all laugh, except for him; he even tells them to shut up, pretending to follow my explanation with attention.

For her part, Irene glowers at me. Provocatively, despite her drooping eyelid. I look away, but she's always there, eyes riveted, regulating the other girls' giggles and whispers.

The wretches complete their worksheets quickly, free of mistakes. I soon run out of exercises to give them and have to improvise other activities, which are neither interesting nor clever.

They take notes and demand more, insatiable, animal, hungry for my humiliation. They know it's all I have to give them.

WEDNESDAY, DECEMBER 13TH

Today in last period, a bird smashed into the window and dropped heavily to the grass. The noise brought the class to a halt. We went to the window to see. The bird was badly injured, its neck snapped, beak half-open. We couldn't tell if it was still alive. We shut the windows, not so much to avoid witnessing the creature's agony, but to keep out the freezing wind that infiltrated the classroom.

We resumed the day's exercises, but my chest was tight with anguish.

Later, I saw the mastiff with the bird in her mouth.

She looked pleased with her prey.

THURSDAY, DECEMBER 14TH

"Tell me, what do García Medrano's papers mean?"

I've run into Gabriela in the hallway and use the opportunity to ask her. She leans on the mop before answering. She bites her lip and this expression would make her look youthful, if it weren't for the bags under her eyes and her dull, washed out skin.

"I don't know what they mean, sir. I started to read them and I didn't understand a thing."

"I'm not surprised, they're incomprehensible . . . but why did you have them?"

She glances around before speaking. The hallway is deserted and none of the security cameras are pointed in our direction.

"I took them from his room when he went away. I had the feeling that if I didn't, someone else would."

"And you held on to them? That's very loyal of you, Gabriela. Why did you give them to me? Do you want me to keep them?"

"No, sir. It's because I don't think he's going to come back."

I take a breath. In another time, this piece of news would have made me happy. Now, I'm not so sure.

"You don't think he's ever coming back?"

"I don't, sir."

"Why? Why is that, Gabriela?"

"I don't know, sir. My intuition. But you can't say anything to anyone."

"Say what? That you think he's gone for good?"

"No, sir. I mean, yes, that too, sir. But I was referring to the papers. No one can know that you have those papers."

"Why not? Is there something bad in them?"

"No, sir. Nothing bad. It's just that . . . they're nobody's business."

She looks down at the floor and I know there's no point in continuing. She won't say anything else, at least not today. She looks wrecked, more resigned than sad, perhaps. As I turn back to my door, she makes a small gesture with her hand. I stop.

"Did you understand any of it, sir?"

"Did I understand any of what?"

"The papers."

"I told you I didn't, Gabriela. I think they're the start of something that was left unfinished. That's all."

"So no, then?"

"No."

She looks disappointed. This is intriguing. Maybe she hoped for some kind of answer, a cracking of a code that had tormented her. I can't give her the satisfaction. I feel an enormous sense of pity. Clumsily, I say:

"Is there something I can do to help, Gabriela?"

She looks at me with faint surprise.

"No, sir. I'm fine, sir. I have everything I need."

FRIDAY, DECEMBER 15TH

I went out for a walk this evening. After all, walking is the only thing I do that isn't imposed on me; my small, insignificant act of freedom. Not even Martínez—elated over his new haul of booze—could make me change my plans.

I preferred to be alone.

Maybe that was a mistake.

It was bitter cold. Frost had accumulated, glittering on the grass. Even the mastiff was reluctant to join me. Mist puffed from her enormous muzzle as she sheltered under the portico at the building's entrance. She watched me pass, unfazed.

I rounded the paddleball courts and continued down the dirt path that led to the opposite wing of the *colich*. From there, I followed the border fence again, walking the length of it for a long time, as the evening darkness deepened.

I'd never gone so far.

I stepped carefully, watching my feet like an inmate pacing a prison yard. That was when I saw the hole in the fence, low to the ground but wide enough to crawl through. Almost without thinking, I crossed to the other side, dragging my coat through the mud.

The smell of the woods hit me immediately.

I moved deeper still, pine needles crackling on the damp earth with my every step. I heard a faint rustling, rodents scurrying or nearby insects, dry pinecones skittering on the ground as I passed. The air was incredibly pure. The solitude, unsettling. It should have been pleasant but wasn't. A cold breeze whirled through the trees and struck me plain in the chest. I felt dizzy, my surroundings were blurred, smudged. I staggered in the direction of the thicket.

I walked for a long time. The sun would set soon but I'd heard the sound of running water and needed to see where it was coming from. I moved deeper into the trees, obsessed, blind, until a tawny owl flew right in front of my face, bringing me to my senses.

I was suddenly aware that I could get lost.

I turned back, reaching the fence at last. Desperate, I started to inspect it, looking for the hole again. Darkness distorted the shape of things, and it took me longer than expected to find the gap. Once I did, I passed through and returned to the path, relieved.

The *colich* looked familiar, safe.

Night had fallen but I could still see the shapes of the buildings, lit by large floodlights. Even with my poor eyesight, I could make them out.

That's how I know I wasn't mistaken.

Marieta was on the assistant headmaster's porch. He was holding her, and she let him. They didn't see me. They couldn't have, even if they looked straight at me. I was in the shadows, and they were lit dimly by the light that spilled through the open door onto the threshold. The contrast would have blinded them.

My stomach turned.

I should have fled from what I was seeing, but I was paralyzed. I watched, squinting to see better, to overcome the vertigo. Their embrace was clumsy and artificial. Lecherous, and lustful, too. He fondled her and she swayed gently against him. They looked like they were in a hurry.

I was hot, all of a sudden. Sweating like a pig, overcome with frustration and resentment.

He pulled her inside the house and closed the door. I waited several minutes more, rooted as if by magnetic force. I heard a whine at my side. It was the mastiff. The dog seemed to be waiting for me to take action. Her brown eyes looked at me, questioningly.

But I didn't know what to do.

I struck her hard and she fled with a whimper.

SATURDAY, DECEMBER 16TH

The hours tick by and I'm locked in my room. I read García Medrano's papers again, his words echoing in my brain, a suggestion of something I'd seen before but not quite understood.

FOUR BY FOUR. Her little world. The girl takes another walk around, goes to bed, gets up. Waits.

Sometimes they open the door. It's usually to leave her food, good food served on plastic plates with small plastic utensils . . .

Like the girl in the story, I'll eat in here today. Confined to my cell.

I don't have the strength to speak to anyone.

I had always known it would be impossible to win Marieta's affections.

I'm not even sure that it matters. She's too twisted, too rigid for me. I don't know how to explain it.

But it's proof, evidence rubbed in my face, that there is no such thing as uncontaminated love.

Marieta must have overcome her distaste for the assistant headmaster, selling herself to him. I can't accept that she's actually attracted to him. They barter with love, with desire. Their minds have adapted to fit that blueprint; they deform their natural impulses and make them monstrous.

Ceding to power, power expands: one plus one is always one more.

The rest of us are left out of this equation.

We add nothing. We take nothing away.

SUNDAY, DECEMBER 17TH

I expected it would be a tiresome, unsurprising Sunday, but that wasn't the case: instead, Crazy Lola turned up out of the blue. I have no idea how she found out I was here. My sister was under strict instructions not to tell her anything, no matter what. But somehow, she'd figured it out.

I was dozing in my room when the phone rang. On the other end of the line, the same voice that usually summons me said simply:

"You have a visitor, Señor Bedragare."

Her tone was pointed, the way she pronounced the end of *señor*. I feared the worst. I rushed out, poorly dressed. And even though *the worst* wasn't waiting for me in the lobby, I wasn't happy with what I saw.

Crazy Lola, with a wicked look in her eye. She was leaning against the wall and biting her lip as if to hold back laughter. She looked good: her hair pulled back, her eyes made up, a tight, revealing knit dress.

"What are you doing here?" I sputtered.

She smiled. "What do you think? I came to see you."

"But who told you, who . . ."

I grabbed her arm and we went out onto the grounds. I thought fewer people would see us there, but the boys were playing soccer on one side of the wall, the girls and their volleyball net on the other. They watched us with curiosity, whispering and giggling.

Crazy Lola was gorgeous, as usual, but I sensed her uneven steps, the psychological instability that tainted everything—even the way she walked.

I asked her again. She didn't answer. She silenced me, throwing herself at me and planting a kiss on my lips.

"Lola, behave yourself," I said.

She laughed.

We sat on a bench under a trellis. I couldn't get her to say how she'd gotten there: she doesn't have a car, not even a driver's license. I also couldn't ascertain why she was here. I gripped her shoulders, looked her in the eye, and spoke as if lecturing a small child:

"You don't want me to lose this job, right?"

The question annoyed her. She stopped laughing and made a face. How could she make me lose my job? Was she not good enough for me? Was I embarrassed of her?

"We're through, Lola. You know that."

It sounded like something out of a *telenovela*, but it was true. Let's remember, she was the one who threw me out on the street.

What did she want now? To act like nothing had happened?

She talked and I had no idea what the hell she was saying. She was offering me a new life, a renewed life, something like that—*revived,* she said—but didn't provide any details.

Was she trying to get back together, now that she knew I finally had a job? Was I no longer useless to her, a "piece of shit wannabe writer"? As she teased apart her tangled argument, waving her small ring-covered hands in feigned frivolity, nibbling on a lock of hair like a girl on a pinup poster, Martínez appeared out of nowhere.

I had to pretend. I said she was a friend and he looked her up and down appreciatively. Would she be staying for lunch? he asked. We could take his car and go to a nearby inn on the road to Cárdenas that he knew well. Good wine, good food, he vehemently described.

"No, no, no," I babbled. "I don't think it's a good idea."

"Why not?" Crazy Lola asked. "I would really like that."

"Because it's late," I interrupted. "I have things to do. I don't like surprises."

"Oh, but I love being surprised! Let's go! Please!"

Martínez followed our conversation closely. Eyes shining and spit gathering in the corners of his mouth. Crazy Lola was worked up, she clapped her hands, showed her excitement.

The decision had been made and there was little I could do. Let them have at it.

They left together. I watched them zigzag away, avoiding the puddles, until they reached Martínez's minivan. He helped her in. She bent over excessively getting into her seat.

The word *jealousy* isn't sufficient for summing up what I felt. In order to be jealous, an intact sense of hope is even more important than love. But in my case, hopelessness is the constant. I admit, however, I did feel something akin to when I witnessed the assistant headmaster groping Marieta: left out and irreversibly depressed.

The same feeling, more or less. One right after the other.

I went back to my room, locked the door, and swore never to ask Martínez or let him tell me about it. Under no circumstance.

MONDAY, DECEMBER 18TH

And yet, he's hard to shut up. He comes over during breakfast, arrogant, carrying a tray loaded with sweets and fruit. He takes the seat next to me despite my obvious rebuff.

"Some friend you have, Bedragare."

"Oh yeah?"

"A real woman from head to toe. She knows how to enjoy a meal and good wine, hold a conversation, and she's . . . totally off her rocker."

"Wow."

"Really fun, really very fun . . ."

Then he turns to me, pretending to be puzzled.

"You're not upset, are you? Don't go thinking there was anything special between us. I'm too old for that sort of thing. I brought her home after we ate. That was it."

"Oh, you don't have to explain anything to me," I reply.

I believe him. I doubt that anything else happened beyond what Martínez was telling me. He wouldn't be able to keep it to himself.

Still, I'm furious. I teach my classes, not bothering to hide my bad mood: the students are perplexed, but they don't shrink before my shouting. They've probably figured it out: the woman they saw me with yesterday rejected me. I won't disabuse them of their opinion. I'm humbled by despair.

TUESDAY, DECEMBER 19TH

I was supervising study hall when there was a disturbance out on the playing fields. All the students left class to look, leaving their notebooks scattered and laptops open.

Consu tried to restrain the two scholarship students she was tutoring, but they too stood up and craned their necks to see better, the shouts registering in their unfathomable eyes.

"What the hell . . ." Consu said from the window, hand held like a visor above her eyes, her face wrinkled in disgust.

I looked out, too, but I could only see heads gathered in little cliques, clouds of dust kicked up around them.

Screams of terror.

We went out.

I heard the words first, then saw the images; both were filled with blood and mangled flesh.

Someone had cut off Lux's head and stuck it on top of one of the paddle court posts. The animal's purpled tongue lolled in his mouth, his eyes open and glassy. Threads of a blackish, bloody substance seeped from the hewn neck.

His body was found a ways off, legs very stiff and the first of the large flies buzzing around his belly. His spine was crushed. He had likely been beaten first and then decapitated.

The girl who had made the discovery was releasing evenly sequenced, theatrical shrieks. Consu led her away to the infirmary. The others, meanwhile, couldn't stop looking, moving closer and closer to take in all the details.

Many of them snapped pictures with their cell phones.

WEDNESDAY, DECEMBER 20TH

Señor J. stopped me as I was coming out of the library. It had been a long time since I'd seen him, even at a distance. Martínez had told me that he was spending time away from the *colich*, but he didn't know where. Now, under that reigning atmosphere of fear and death, the headmaster had reappeared, looking at me with his signature indolence.

He invited me for a drink.

Unease and alarm on my part, but I didn't have any choice but to accept.

I followed him to the enormous living room where I had first seen him, and where I hadn't visited since.

He fixed me a dry martini and sat facing me in a wingback chair, crossing his legs, solicitous and very serious.

He watched me for a long time in silence. I had nothing to say, either.

The fireplace warmed the room and lit his face with a golden glow. A Christmas tree was set in the corner, decorated with ornaments of silver and sky blue. Tiny bulbs blinked on and off, following alternating patterns that I tried to decipher, killing time.

He started to talk, of course, about the assistant headmaster's cat. Yes, it was obviously an attack on the assistant headmaster's person, he impassively stated. The assistant headmaster was very close to that little pet—that's what he said, "that little pet," stressing the t's—in any case, it wouldn't be easy to determine who had perpetrated the attack. The assistant headmaster was investigating and Marieta had helped him with the interviews. They were especially focused on the Goon and Ignacio's group, but nothing had come of it yet, nothing specific at least.

I expected Señor J. to ask my opinion, but in his mind the matter was already closed: he wasn't the least bit interested. In fact, he seemed almost satisfied.

"Ignacio? He wouldn't waste his time," he chuckled, changing the subject with a wave of his hand.

No, he had brought me there for another reason. He furrowed his brow and asked about Crazy Lola.

I sipped my martini slowly before answering. I fumbled for the right response, unsure if he asked out of curiosity or reproach.

Seeing my hesitation, he hurried to add:

"Of course, anyone who wants to visit you is welcome."

I smiled, playing the fool.

"I wasn't expecting her visit. She's an old friend; I hadn't heard from her in a long time. I was the first to be surprised, seeing her here. I hope it wasn't a problem."

"Of course not. It was good she came on a Sunday, when there's nothing to interrupt. I saw her sitting with you on the bench, and I saw her leave with old Martínez. Very beautiful girl, your friend."

I nodded sadly, casting my eyes around the room. Valuable-looking trinkets were arranged in a glass case: African carvings, a pair of religious figurines, urns with gold inlay. The word *plunder* came to mind. A framed shadow box displaying a string of pinned butterflies hung on the wall.

I really had no idea of how to continue the conversation.

Señor J. served me another martini and scooted his chair a little closer to the sofa where I sat.

Then out it came. All of it.

The exchange was ambiguous, murky, and though I believe I understood his meaning perfectly at the time, I find I'm incapable of reproducing it. I don't even really remember how it started, or how it developed. Several precise details stick in my mind: Señor J.'s tongue and gums, the glint of the fire off the heavy iron poker, the distant whine of the mastiff, the intoxicating smell of charred firewood.

Like the butterflies pinned in their box, those insignificant details are fixed in place while the overall conversation—so significant—comes back to me suffused with a sense of unreality.

But the conversation happened. It was real.

We talked about women, or rather, he talked about women, but not women, really, because what he talked about was sex.

He assumed I had needs but was embarrassed to confess them.

Magnanimous, he let me know that he was a man of the world, a tolerant man, and that he was drawn to contemplating evil head-on, as the ineluctable complement to good, without moral connotations.

I thought he was simply philosophizing. I nodded and told him that I, too, was interested in the contemplation of evil, under the exact premises he described.

In truth, I would have agreed with any thesis he proposed. I just wanted to escape as soon as possible, escape victorious, having said and done the right thing.

The fire spit. Señor J. added a few more logs and poked at it indifferently.

I believe it was then that he started to talk to me about the girls.

He told me there were girls at our disposal, if we required them.

I babbled. I wanted to think he was joking.

"Girls?" I said.

"Well, to call them girls is a bit of an exaggeration," he said. "They're all of age, and are more than experienced, of course. We're not spoiling any apples. Quite the contrary: we remove them from the bushel before they spoil the rest."

It took me a while to realize that he was serious. Why was he telling me something so private? The situation might have been legal, but it could undoubtedly ruin anyone's reputation, especially the headmaster of a well-heeled boarding school.

Or maybe he was testing me, intending to unnerve, to piss on his territory and watch me tremble, bound hand and foot, obliged to smile, nod, accept?

I didn't try to argue. I only managed to ask for details, which he was happy to give. No, the girls didn't have a direct relationship to the *colich*. The odd one might have been a former student, perhaps, but always from the groups of scholarship students, those girls who were already corrupted when they arrived, unable to keep up with the others. Sometimes they had boys, too. The offer is as varied as the demand, he added.

Abuse, beatings, drug addiction, alcoholism: they could be saved from all that, thanks to the *colich*. It's a simple trade, a healthy, hygienic exchange in which both parties benefit; this exchange has always existed, no point in denying it.

He was smiling. His words had a clean, reasonable texture.

"But where are they?" I asked. "Do they live here?"

"No, no of course not. Sometimes they spend a few days, no more. Then we use the opportunity to help them a bit. We give them money, food, clothes, even letters of recommendation if possible."

He shrugged. "We can't do any more than that."

The conversation was shifting: it seemed we were no longer discussing bodies and exchange, but a kind of solidarity, a concern for those kids who—from time to time—came to visit Wybrany. Señor J.'s points sounded sensible, irrefutable.

What was left for me to say? Was Señor J. about to offer me something? Martínez had told me he was addicted to cocaine. Was he going to offer me a line? A girl? Both? I got up to go, and all he offered was another dry martini.

"The last one," he said.

I turned it down. I could feel the alcohol, bitter and dry, burning my throat. I'd had enough. Señor J. saw me to the door, somewhat peevishly. I was unsteady. I wobbled across the grounds, imagining lecherous shadows behind every bush. The night was pitch black. Everyone was already in their rooms, doing God knows what.

I shuddered.

The mastiff walked with me the whole way back. Her fur was damp. She looked up at me, her eyes liquid and mute. She didn't seem to remember the smack I'd given her the other day. I scratched her ears and said I was sorry. Then I went to my room.

THURSDAY, DECEMBER 21ST

The morning dawned sunny and cold. Outside, the lawn sparkled, but my nightmares hadn't faded.

Between dreams and flashes of wakefulness, I had been reliving that conversation all night. García Medrano's papers suddenly made sense. They came to me—dead cats, fire pokers, tearful children, lines of cocaine. I was unable to reject anything I was offered. I drank, snorted, fornicated with apathy, devoid of desire.

I woke feeling nauseous. I looked outside: at first glance, nothing seemed any different.

But that wasn't the case; in fact, the entire *colich* was in festive spirits. The hallways, dining hall, veranda, all had been decorated for Christmas, an ill-timed scene in a Nordic theme: reindeer, snow, golden pinecones, fir trees. Not at all original.

The kids were more relaxed, too. Classes ran smoothly, they completed their exercises without complaint. I observed each and every one of them, seeing them with new eyes. What did they know, how much did they know, why did they keep quiet? They looked up and returned my gaze, surprised, perhaps, by the scrutiny. I sat stiffly, huddled in my seat. My hands shook and my eyes burned. I'm sure they must have noticed.

(. . .)

I try to put aside my resentment of Martínez and go looking for him in the afternoon. I find him on the bleachers, cheering on the boys in a special pre-Christmas soccer match being held for some kind of charitable cause. I approach him covertly, despite the hubbub. Maybe he thinks that I want to talk about Crazy Lola, because he stiffens and flushes slightly. From pride, not shame.

But he can tell straight away that I have something else on my mind.

I try not to be obvious.

Señor J. didn't say it was a secret, but still, I prefer to be cautious. I drop hints, one or two telling words.

Martínez stares straight ahead. He appears not to have heard me, but it's an act. He's listening, and he catches on right away. He doesn't say a word either in favor or against, but he gives himself away with a smile. I ask for details. He restricts himself to watching me from the corner of his eye, watching the game unfolding below. Then he turns, shrugs, and mutters vagaries.

His passiveness angers me. I raise my voice, call him out.

"Don't judge lest ye be judged," he says.

"I'm not judging! I'm just trying to understand. Everyone seems to be part of something I'm not. I always feel excluded."

A light sparks in his eyes; his expression changes.

"You want to join in? You?"

"I don't want to join in. I just want to *know*. How hard is that to understand, Martínez? I want to be looped in on the rules."

Martínez shakes his head. He seems annoyed, all of a sudden. He's winded. With his hands resting on his knees, back hunched, he looks like a broken man, older than usual.

"Nobody knows the rules. That's a fact of life."

"I don't believe you. Someone makes the rules, someone must know them."

We fall quiet. The game continues to stir up the crowd. The boys play well, they shine with health and happiness. Even Ignacio, ordinarily so weak, looks better today. He runs up and down the field, hiding his limp, getting passes he isn't always able to trap. No one dares call him out over a bad shot; he is either feared or worshipped by all the boys. A gimpy leader, I think, or a leading gimp. Not much of a difference.

The sun is setting. I get up without saying goodbye. Martínez has already given me everything I need from him.

(. . .)

Knowledge weighs heavy on me and I want to get to the bottom of things. I want to see what the others see. I want to ask all of them. I want to know why they stay quiet. I want to know.

I try Ledesma. I look for him everywhere, but he can't be found. I don't know how he spends his free time. Only occasionally have I seen him wandering by himself—like me—through the grounds or hallways, classroom to classroom, eyes downcast.

Like me, he must spend a lot of time in his room.

I decide to knock on his door for the first time. I need courage to show up unannounced, but he opens his door like nothing is out of the ordinary and steps aside for me to come in.

Ledesma's room is stark, bare; there's hardly a trace of him there. Music that sounds like old Tracia *cantos* pours from his laptop, a sad, deep melody. There are no books or papers on his desk. His room is defined more by emptiness than order. He sits down on the bed and looks at me without a hint of curiosity.

I speak more clearly this time.

Yes, he says. It's as bad as I fear or worse. It's been happening for about three or four years. There is nothing I can do to change it. These are the new rules of the game.

"Again with the damn rules," I whisper.

I know what the world is like. I haven't lived my life in a bubble. I know decadence, I know evil, chaos. But it should have been different here. One had assumed this place was different; a refuge for civilization, an oasis.

Ledesma, head bowed, listens and smiles. Despite the cold, he wears only pajama pants and an undershirt that shows his ribs. He's thin, drawn. I see him and I see the scars on his arms, too. He raises his eyes and notices me studying him. His expression doesn't change.

He talks to me about Señor J.'s decisions. The great developer, Ledesma calls him. He realized some years ago that Wybrany's isolation had a flip side. One escapes the external evils, certainly, but monsters are generated inside these walls. Castration, amputation, pain. Ledesma tells me about a certain Celia, a scholarship girl. She set all of this off, he says. Suicide, that's how it ended.

"Few people know that, very few," he murmurs.

But he will reveal all. He no longer fears for himself, he assures me. They were able to pass the girl's disappearance off as an expulsion; she'd been rather disobedient, in the end, and had tried to run away before.

"The assistant headmaster said it was extortion, blackmail. Those were his words. The girl had manipulated him from the beginning, in exchange for certain favors, and well, things got out of hand . . ."

"What are you talking about? What got out of hand?"

"The corruption spread, everything became tainted, everywhere. More and more people became involved. Maybe she really did start it . . . but later he couldn't control himself. He even brought friends here; he wanted to share her, show off his possession. The girl slit her wrists the day before the school year started. There was blood everywhere when they found her, little could be done."

"And am I supposed to believe that no one noticed? That no one made the connection? No one demanded that somebody take the blame?"

Ledesma shifts on the bed, stretches his legs. He appears to consider this.

"The blame?" he says at last. "No, not exactly. There was a power shift, a change of hands. That's how things work here. And as for the connection being made . . . it doesn't matter. Pointless, unless the conclusions drawn were to be spoken aloud. This is easier for some to handle than others."

He looks up. His voice is changing.

"The silence, you know. Some handle it better than others. It depends on what one gets in exchange. Peace of mind, or a deal."

Now I know what he means by "deal." Those transactions created to paper over each new disaster. The cancer that spreads through the *colich*. To know and not say, to speak without words.

The best way to avoid chaos is to build a channel where it can flow in secret.

"An underground channel," he concludes.

Ledesma is taciturn, his eyes roam the room. He's losing steam. Maybe he regrets revealing so much. He hesitates, blanching, an ironic smile playing on his lips. Martínez had been more agile, less talkative. Everything had been summed up by his question: "*You want to join in? You?*"

Tracia's laments have finished playing and we hear only the murmur of our own breathing: the others must already be at dinner; we've missed the start.

I stand to go, but Ledesma stops me.

"Do you remember what I told you about García Medrano?"

I give a distracted nod. He wraps his arms around his body.

"He killed himself, too. Your predecessor. This is also a secret, supposedly. They won't acknowledge the suicides, but there have been several. Enough to paint this place in a bad light."

"How do you know this?" I ask.

"Gabriela saw him. She told me. Ask her. But be very careful. Knowledge can drive you straight to madness."

FRIDAY, DECEMBER 22ND

Today, the students received their first trimester grades and prepared to go home for the holiday break.

Christmas Eve is the day after tomorrow. Their cheeks are rosy and their movements hurried. Parents began arriving at midday to collect their children. The administration turned out to greet them. From my window, I saw Señor J.: arrogant, posh, shaking hands left and right. The assistant headmaster, still battered from the death of his cat, all saccharine smiles, hunched, pliant, submissive; Marieta, both distant and close, hot and cold. Attractive. Hateful.

The students pour out of the hall pulling expensive suitcases behind them, in their long dress coats and plaid scarves. They look like little executives, embryos of future commanders, presumptuous, fatuous. They look straight ahead; they don't even squint in the sunlight. Even Ignacio holds himself elegantly today; he has turned his limp into something distinctive, a more authoritative way to step on the world. His mother looks surprised when she sees him, gives him an unpracticed embrace. She embarrasses him and he rebuffs her, looking for complicity in his classmates.

They leave and only the few scholarship students remain. They picked up their grades with the neutrality of their station, neither ashamed nor resigned, biting their lips with pride.

There was a girl crying today, a girl named Marcela, hairy and gypsy-looking, with close-set eyes. I think she's the youngest daughter of one of the drivers. Why was she crying? It was whispered that she had to leave the *colich*. Her marks had been abysmal. I myself had given her a failing grade. Her classmates didn't even bother trying to console her. By a wide margin, Marcela is the worst student in her year.

A thought flitted across my mind, settling in the pit of my stomach. I wanted to erase it, but there it remained, lodged. It can't be, I tell myself, it can't be.

Marcela is fifteen years old.

(. . .)

The hours pass and I'm still watching out the window at the parade of fathers, mothers, hellos, smiles, Señor J., the assistant headmaster, Marieta, the kids, the setting sun, manners, and artifice, shaking hands with such elegance.

I feel a bit unwell. I don't know what to do with myself.

My colleagues will all go somewhere for the holidays. No one is expected to spend Christmas Eve here except the workers, who have to stay on to look after the facilities. I haven't been told that I'm obliged to leave. Neither has anyone asked where I plan to go. There is a kind of tacit agreement not to pry in such affairs, which suddenly seem banal, almost obscene. Who knows, maybe Martínez is staying at the *colich* and doesn't want to admit it; maybe Ledesma will hole up in a roadside motel; maybe Sacra is desperately calling all of her city friends who have already decamped for holiday resorts, changed their numbers, invented excuses not to invite her.

Time, ineluctable, ticks by. Our lives are nothing more than a succession of lies and appearances.

We all play a role and it's only the nuances in our performance that define us.

The trouble is, I still don't know whom I will play.

For the time being, I'm in my room. Vulnerable. The recent days seem like a dream, a bad dream, all the turbidity of a nightmare.

I face the mirror and am met with the very image of fatigue: a face tinged green, unshaven, sunken eyes, shadows marking my cheekbones, defeated shoulders, despondent.

TUESDAY, DECEMBER 26TH

I wander the halls of the *colich*, my footsteps echoing on the tiled floor even when I walk slowly. There are shadows, ghosts, desolation here. It's cold. The wind lashes the trees: the storm ripped down several branches. No one has bothered to remove them from the paths.

But still, it's quiet. In contrast with where I've just been, which is ruled by chaos and noise.

I wasn't brave enough to stay at the *colich* by myself, obviously. I gave in and called my sister, the poor thing. Having her is like having no one, in the end.

I went to her apartment. We were alone, the two of us, feeling more besieged than celebratory. She had gone to great lengths to prepare a nice meal, the typical Christmas Eve roast, plus shellfish, candied fruit, *turrón*, champagne. I think she'd even gone to the salon. Her hair was soft and spongy, and she patted it constantly.

We ate with barely a word, the television on, trying to pretend everything was normal, reminiscing sporadically over idealized childhood memories.

My sister asked how my novel was coming along. I briefly considered my answer.

"Fine," I said. "It's about a mystery."

"What mystery?"

"A mystery about rules that are established but never completely defined. The stranger doesn't know them. He can't come to terms with them, even if he wanted to. But he can't fight them, either. The rules exist. They're strong, unquestionable, but they're not written anywhere. Therefore, they can't be obeyed or disobeyed."

She wrinkled her forehead as if she understood, but she was obviously confused. She stood and plugged in the lights on a plastic wreath. Then she sat back down.

"And what are these rules about?"

"I'm not sure yet. That's why it's a mystery novel. I'm finding out as I write."

"Are there murders?"

"Yes, there are," I concluded. "One decapitation, at least."

She shuddered. She seemed satisfied.

(. . .)

The ruckus in the street was deranged and didn't even end with the dawn. It was more than just laughter and singing drunks—there were shouts, too, and cries for help that went unanswered. I slept—tried to sleep—on the pull-out couch. Headlights from passing cars projected beams of light on the walls, passing from one side of the living room to the other.

I barely slept.

In the morning, still half asleep, I called Crazy Lola. I still don't know why. Maybe I couldn't stand the thought of staying longer at my sister's house, of having lunch together and all the rest. But Lola didn't pick up, not then and not the five or six times I tried again over the course of the day. Anguish stabbed me in the gut with each unanswered call.

(. . .)

Our Christmas lunch was comprised of leftovers from the night before and two bottles of wine that we drank slowly and which put me to sleep for the whole afternoon. Calmer now, the street below pulsed with a dampened din, a slow boil.

We looked at old photos. My sister always brings out the photo album on these occasions. I have it memorized. She does, too, but it doesn't seem to matter. She points to the pictures with her bony finger and makes unsubstantial comments.

I see her as a little girl, I see myself as a little boy, I see my parents when they were children, I see people who have died, people I knew, people I only think of when I see them in the album and invariably forget once it's closed.

From the corner of one photograph, an adolescent looks out at me sadly. He isn't the subject of the photo; his presence is a mistake but there he is with his astonished eyes and bony little body. For an instant, I focus on the image and scrutinize the picture, looking for myself.

Is it me?

(. . .)

I was able to sleep a bit the second night, despite the fact that there was an even greater commotion outside, if that's possible. Someone was throwing a party down at street level. A group of beggars had set up their pieces of cardboard and rags to spend the night. Dance music ricocheted off the walls. I think things ended badly. I heard a police car, broken glass, an ambulance. I also heard my sister snoring. She must be used to this.

When morning came, I left her a note on the kitchen table and drove the deserted highway back to Wybrany. I experienced a sharp sense of homecoming upon reaching the little road that runs through the woods.

I passed the darkened fields. At the end of the road the *colich* buildings rose in a final flourish. The flags crowning the lecture building waved weakly. The silence was soothing after so much noise and I breathed it in like it was fresh air.

No one was expecting me. I stood at the gate, shivering with cold and ringing the bell until Brito, one of the scholarship boys, came to open up. Brito is mulish and stocky. He has a wide jaw and lovely, distrustful eyes.

I asked him, blushing, who was around.

"Just us, sir."

I didn't know who he meant by *us*, whether or not *us* also included me. Is *us* a category reserved for the scholarship students and their parents; for *colich* workers and their children? Do I count as *us*? *Us* clearly doesn't include Señor J., the assistant headmaster, or Marieta. So where can we find ourselves, those in the middle, in neither camp? The upstarts, loners, imposters like me?

In any case, we must have been few. I didn't come across anyone in the hall, though I did hear muffled voices behind a few doors. The dining room was closed. I peeked into the kitchen. Gabriela and another woman were going to great lengths to deep clean the fume hoods. They showed no surprise at seeing me. Gabriela might have looked slightly uncomfortable, but not surprised.

"We can bring your meals to your room, sir," they told me. "If you let us know in advance."

Yes, I would let them know. And maybe if I was lucky and Gabriela brought me my food, I could ask her about García Medrano and the girls. I already knew. Ledesma had told me. She only had to give me her opinion. She had no reason to feel forced into revealing anything. She shouldn't be afraid.

I holed up in my room after an afternoon walk. Night soon fell. Unfortunately, it was Merche who brought me dinner.

The wind rattles the shutters. It's cold out. Inside, the heat adds a soft, sickly quality to the air.

WEDNESDAY, DECEMBER 27TH

When I was returning from my walk today, I thought I saw a man pulling a crying girl by the hand.

It was getting dark and my eyesight has worsened, but one thing is clear: whoever the man was (by his height and shape it could have been the assistant headmaster, though his gait was different, and he wasn't dressed like himself) and whoever the girl was (a girl who was just starting to grow into something else), the pair made their way unevenly, jerking along without speaking. They disappeared around the corner in a hurry.

I was curious and wanted to follow them, but I quickly decided against it.

Then, from outside, I saw a light in the hallway of one of the warehouses, illuminating the branches of the tree at the entrance. A dark bird, maybe a blackbird, flew away. The light went out. After a few minutes, it came on again. I heard the sound of a door abruptly slamming shut.

I got out of there before I could be accused of spying.

The buildings are hushed, now. There are hardly any lights on and the only sound is a motor running, maybe the heat or the kitchen exhaust.

Merche told me in the dining hall that she and Gabriela are taking turns at lunch, but apart from Merche herself, the boy who opened the gate, and Tato, the concierge, I haven't met anyone else in two days.

THURSDAY, DECEMBER 28TH

I wake with a fever and aching bones and almost faint when I sit up in bed. The room is cold, but my body burns.

I'm still experiencing certain sensations from my dream, which I vainly try to piece together. I only remember that it had been tender and sensual, someone lightly stroking my crotch. The tingling I felt went far beyond the purely sexual; it was something spiritual, or metaphysical.

And yet, all I have at this moment is a persistent—almost insolent—erection.

Accumulating blood that only adds to my dizziness.

I touch my forehead. It's on fire. I feel my way for a glass of water. As I drink, I notice my lips are very swollen, ready to burst.

My brain swirls with meaningless words. I think I hear a voice calling me by my name—my real name. It's my imagination. I try to calm down.

I get back in bed and enter a state of drowsiness, a not at all pleasant semi-consciousness which lasts almost the entire morning.

I think that I'm going to die like this, completely alone in this isolated room. I don't care. No one is waiting for me. I don't have children, I don't have parents. My responsibility to my sister is purely functional.

(. . .)

In the afternoon, I remember I have a bottle of aspirin in the closet. I go to get it, using the wall for support. I take two and then pee. My urine is dark and smells of infection. I fall immediately back to sleep.

I have another dream. This time Marcela, with her brown, fuzzy little face, whines and asks me for water. *I don't have any water, Marcela,* I answer, *I'm really thirsty too and there isn't even any water for me.* She keeps complaining, her face grows thin, suddenly she's old and turns into something closer to my sister than a young girl.

As in my dream, I need to drink something when I wake up. I take little sips so I don't vomit. I also take two more aspirin. I think they help. My fever has gone down a bit.

I look out the window. It's night already. Stars twinkle in the clear sky. After many windy days, the air is calm and the moonlight shines gently on the stone façades. I must have slept for eight hours straight and I haven't eaten anything all day. The very thought of food makes me indescribably nauseous.

In any case, even if I wanted to call down to the dining hall, dinner is over.

I am utterly alone.

SATURDAY, DECEMBER 30TH

I've been very sick. I still am, three days later, but I'm now starting to recover.

I slump at my desk, my body heavier than usual, and focus on scrawling in my notebook.

I spent all of yesterday in bed, basically unconscious. I only dragged myself up to use the bathroom. I lost all sense of time. I was cold, and hot. My teeth chattered. I sweat. I ran out of aspirin. I didn't even drink any water.

My mind flipped through a series of images. One after another, those slides projecting on a screen. I observed them, unfazed. A new image would emerge only when the previous one had faded away. Crazy Lola. My ex-brother-in-law. My signature forged on his papers. My parents. The factory line where I worked for so many years. The assistant headmaster, his cat in his arms. The cat, without its head. The assistant headmaster's hands on Marieta's ass. Marieta sipping tea. The mastiff running in the woods. The photograph of the puny adolescent I had been once. Ignacio with a furrowed brow. Irene licking her lips. A girl pulled along by an unknown man. Gabriela with García Medrano's papers under her arm. Gabriela peering through the crack in my door.

This last image had been real, I found out, although it had the same pale, confused texture of dreams.

Having knocked several times to no avail, Gabriela grew concerned and decided to open the door to see if I was okay.

She found me in bed, wet and reeking, a prisoner of hallucinations and fever dreams.

"Sir! What's wrong?"

Her words were sweetness itself. If that voice was coming from my unconscious, I didn't want to wake.

But Gabriela shook me gently, touched my forehead, her eyes wide with shock. She ran from the room, then returned with medicine and covered me with cool rags.

The memories that flood me have a strange consistency: Gabriela's touch, her smell and her voice, are still absolutely clear, hyperreal, while the passage of time, space, and other physical shapes dissipate completely. I had entered a purely sensorial fetal-like state, overcome by fever and the relief of being cared for, stripped of intelligence and reason.

I fell in love with Gabriela.

I know she managed to lift me from the bed: I remember the squeak of a wheelchair. I know she bathed me: I remember the bubbles, the penetrating smell of soap. I know she fed me: I remember the glint on the approaching spoon, the tepid concoction sliding down my throat.

I don't remember any doctor coming to see me.

Nor do I remember the night or the dawn. I don't remember the arrival of morning with its light and sound.

I do remember Gabriela at my side, making coffee. Dissolving a little packet in a glass of water.

(. . .)

I'm awake after a long nap. Conscious at last.

There's no one here now. Gabriela will bring me dinner, I hope, and I'll able to thank her properly.

My heart is beating in anticipation. I feel entirely changed. I struggle to get up and look at myself in the mirror. A pale, thin face looks back in surprise. I've aged.

SUNDAY, DECEMBER 31ST

My sister just called. She couldn't wait any longer, she says. I left so suddenly without telling her, and too many days had passed since she'd heard from me.

Her voice is haughty, demanding. Maddening.

"I didn't leave without telling you! I left you a note!"

"A note? Do you really think a note is sufficient? One, cold note? It's Christmas!"

"Who cares if it's Christmas?"

"I care!"

We're both silent for several seconds. My head hurts. Even the pressure from the phone against my temple is torture.

"Who are you going to spend New Year's Eve with? Are you going to leave me by myself?" she finally says.

"New Year's Eve?"

I hadn't realized what day it was.

I consider using my illness as an excuse, but hold back. She might decide to come see me. I can't think of anything worse. I say I have to stay at the *colich* and be on call.

"On call? You're a teacher, not a doorman. Who'd believe that on call business?"

"Me. I do."

"Well, I think the right thing is for you to come here, with me."

"Right? Now you're going to tell me what's right?"

She starts to whimper.

"Why do you have to talk to me like that? You didn't used to be like this. What's your problem with me?"

I don't respond. I hear her sniveling, distorted by interference. I hang up the phone.

Gabriela is watching me placidly.

"Was that your wife, sir?"

"Oh, no. I'm not married."

It feels good to say it. Not being married suddenly feels very agreeable. She continues to watch me without another word. She doesn't even blink. I don't know if she believes me. I don't know if she doubts. I don't know what she thinks.

I look at her tired face. A deep wrinkle scores her forehead. There are mottled spots on her cheeks. She wears her hair pulled back and I can see a few gray strands peppering her locks. She's older than I am, possibly not by much, but she's seen more. She's wiser. I feel deep tenderness for her.

"What are you doing tonight?" I ask. "Will you have dinner with your daughter?"

She shakes her head.

"No, my daughter is in Cárdenas. She doesn't have a car. She can't come here."

"And you can't go see her?"

"It's hard, sir. She shares an apartment with other girls. There's no room for me. And I don't have a car, either. Someone would have to drive me, and I'd have to sleep in a hotel. All of that costs a lot of money."

"I imagine you must miss her."

"I do, sir. But it's okay. I can't complain."

I think for a moment.

"Would you like to have dinner with me, Gabriela?"

I'm surprised by her quick response. She doesn't hesitate.

"Of course, sir. If you'd like."

I smile and try to hide my enthusiasm. I list my conditions: she'll have to use the informal *you*, stop endlessly calling me *sir*, she mustn't prepare anything special, she doesn't need to serve me.

She nods, reserved. But when she goes to speak, *sir* slips out. She has to stop and think, make an effort. She cuts herself off on the first sound: "s— . . ." almost as if she were struggling against her own nature.

Now I write and wait, while she gets ready for dinner. I've changed out of my pajamas, put on clean clothes, trimmed my nails, shaved, and splashed on cologne. A new year is about to begin. I'm disoriented, unnerved, and still convalescing, but for the first time in a long while, I sense a change. A smile, unbidden, comes to my lips.

Like all the December thirty-firsts of my childhood, I write down my intentions for the new year.

TUESDAY, JANUARY 2ND

Cold. A curdled sun. Gabriela's body, ripe but sweet. We've spent these past days in my room.

She gives herself to me. She's submissive. This makes me uncomfortable because I suspect she doesn't submit to *me* but rather to what she believes I represent: authority, rank.

I wasn't the first. I know that now. I'm substituting for García Medrano in this, as well.

He won't be returning to claim what once belonged to him. Ledesma was right: Gabriela knew. Gabriela told me.

She was the one who found him. The sight of his shoes pointed down at the floor, motionless, when she entered the room. The chair knocked on its side. The little pool of urine. He had been dead for several hours.

This very room.

No one warned me that I'd been sleeping in a cursed room this whole time. The source of my nightmares. My illness, perhaps.

I don't blame her for not saying anything.

She turns away when she tells me. Moonlight bathes her profile, makes her beautiful. I know she feels old, hates her horsey teeth, hates her gray hair. She possesses a muted coquettishness, deeply feminine but rusty from disuse.

I don't compliment her because I don't want her to be embarrassed. She'd think I was lying. And I don't want to lie, either. Not the time for that, anymore. We've entered a new age, one in which the lies that used to make sense no longer do, and the truths that once sustained us begin to disguise themselves as lies. From now on, we will be ruled by other codes, other norms, a hostile environment to which we must adapt in order to survive.

I just want to hold her, feel her close, her deep, sharp smell and tepid warmth.

My fever still crops up in the afternoons, and to soothe its aftereffects, I doze as I listen to her talk, spurred on by my questions. Naturally quiet, she only talks because I oblige her.

She tells me about him and her voice is gentle. I think she loved him, perhaps, or misses him. It's possible to envy a dead man. I know this because I'm jealous: an anxiety that gnaws and tarnishes what should be a pure refuge. And yet, I need to know more. What happened, why he did it.

She doesn't know. I believe she is sincere.

She is thoughtful, then; piecing something back together inside herself. I watch as her lips move soundlessly. Then she speaks.

She remembers that García Medrano had been deeply affected by what happened to Celia. He didn't know how to keep quiet. Maybe suicide was the only path that remained for him.

Celia. The girl who also killed herself, I say.

Gabriela raises herself up on one elbow. She's surprised that I know the story. When it happened, hardly anyone in all of Wybrany knew the truth. And those who did were called to a meeting by Señor J., a meeting in which he made his threat perfectly clear.

"But there are always cracks, always crevices," I say. "You were going to tell me. And Ledesma did, before you could. It was always a matter of time—more time, or less—but all shit floats to the surface in the end."

"It was Ledesma who told you? He's your sort," she says, lying back down. "That's why he couldn't keep quiet. García Medrano, too."

"And what sort is that?" Another lash of jealousy.

Withdrawn, weak, pensive, second-best. Those aren't her words. Gabriela's vocabulary is more concise. She sums up the complexity in one simple expression; she knows how to synthesize, give weight to language: the *from-below* sort, she says.

So above and below still exist, then. Where is Señor J., above or below? And Marieta, Martínez, Sacra? Where is Ignacio? My sister? Crazy Lola? Where is the girl, Marcela?

I utter this final question out loud.

She turns over gently. Touches my forehead, whispers that my fever is back.

I repeat the question. "Where is Marcela?" She pronounces the name slowly: Marcela.

Marcela is with them, she says at last. They took her out of school because she was hopeless. She was never going to learn anything. Now she's with them. She'll stay on at the *colich*, in another way.

Something roils in the pit of my stomach. I remember Señor J.'s account: There are girls at our disposal.

"What do her parents say?" I whisper.

"What can they say? There's nothing they can do. It's not like there are other options."

My eyelids are heavy.

I fight off fatigue, try to concentrate on Gabriela's image. She doesn't even look concerned. Even a compassionate, tender person such as herself can accept the existence of the sewers.

I'm tired.

I don't say anything else and remain motionless, sheltered under the covers.

Gabriela does, too, but she no longer looks at me. She simply closes her eyes and falls silent.

SUNDAY, JANUARY 7TH

The children begin to return, and the teachers, and once again the *colich* fills with sounds that would seem to represent life, but which I now know represent something very different.

Yesterday, I saw Señor J., the assistant headmaster, and Marieta. They were in the dining hall, toasting the New Year with champagne. Marieta wore a green dress, long and low cut, her shoulders exposed. She has a magnificent body. Her skin glows. The assistant headmaster didn't take his eyes off her. In contrast, Señor J. looked above their heads, his eyes at half-mast, a faint, arrogant smile.

They greeted me from their seats. I had no desire to approach them; I sensed that perhaps it wasn't expected of me.

By now, they must know about my relationship with Gabriela. They must know that I've learned my predecessor's fate.

We all know more than we pretend to.

But if they don't tell me and I don't ask, it's as though nothing has happened. That's how sewers work: occasionally, the stench seeps out, we smell it, but the sewers remain below, out of sight, unmentioned. As if they didn't exist.

I nod at the trio's greeting and decide to exaggerate my continuing convalescence. I take only a bowl of soup, shuffle over to a seat with an afflicted air, leave the table quickly, and return to my room. I have played my part in the performance. They pretend to believe it.

I see Martínez entering his room with an enormous suitcase, probably loaded with bottles. Pleased with himself, upbeat, he slaps me hard on the back. I stumble. I tell him I've been very sick and he laughs, unbelieving. His face has deteriorated since I last saw him. I don't know where he spent the holidays. He doesn't say and I don't ask. There's a wrinkle of suffering between his brows, but his chatter wipes it away. I take a more indulgent view of him today: both love and illness have made me more tolerant.

Sacra stops me on the porch. She brings her face very close to mine. Her lipstick is messy and she smells of alcohol.

"You're pale, honey," she says.

In contrast, her skin is flushed, a slick of sweat at her sideburns and above her lip. She asks me where I've been. I give a short, concise response.

"A few days here, a few in Cárdenas."

Then I turn, leaving her at the entrance. I don't bother to fake a reason for my rudeness.

Back to the norm, Gabriela has a full workday again. She can only come to me at night. She always comes in secret. I wait, impatient. She comes with her head bowed, a rushed expression. She's keeping up appearances.

I, on the other hand, have reached the point at which I couldn't care less. I don't even have an interest in pretending to be a decent teacher.

I've to come to understand that—here—certain things don't exist and aren't a danger to anyone, so long as they're left undefined by words.

MONDAY, JANUARY 8TH

First day of classes in the new year. The students watch me with bold, thuggish little eyes. They all received lots of gifts this Christmas; they bring them to the *colich* and show each other to determine whose is the latest, the most expensive.

Ignacio is back with a new leather jacket and a pair of sunglasses that make him look like a pimp. Irene is wearing long, dangly earrings, necklaces, rings, an entire hardware store on her person. She's heavily made up—shades of red, blue, green spread artlessly over her asymmetrical face.

The whole class period is a celebration of such novelties. I don't try to impose any kind of order. I sit back. Let them do what they want.

The gap Marcela has left is barely noticeable. She never made much noise anyway. No one asks about her. She's been removed from my roster and I don't utter her name, either.

We move on. Seamlessly.

(. . .)

I run into Ledesma in the hallway after class. I haven't seen him since the day we talked in his room. He glances at me sideways and comes over, his head down, briefcase practically dragging on the tiled floor. He just wants to say a brief hello, but I keep him there.

I ask him about Marcela. I want to know what he thinks about the girl.

For the first time, I see distrust in his eyes. He suggests that I know as well as he where she could be.

"Of course I know," I say. "But we're just going to leave it there?"

I peer into his sunken eyes and see only disappointment. A long, endless, empty corridor. I've never seen a look so opaque, so dead.

He responds, drawing out his words.

"Do you really think you can do anything?"

I stammer. He takes a step back, puffs out his chest. He no longer seems worried about appearing disturbed. He speaks, but it's like he's reciting the words. As if someone else were speaking through his mouth.

"All we have left is shame, torrents of shame, rivers and seas of shame. What kind of world is this, where we're told by a madman that we should be ashamed? The greatest evil of our time is that there are no *maestros* left to follow. But we must stop a moment. We must listen to all the hopeless voices."

"I don't understand, Ledesma. What are you talking about?"

"I'm talking about the insects, the insects buzzing. About things that are but are not seen. It doesn't matter if we try to hide them. The eyes of all of humanity are on the pit into which we're poised to fall. But I'm tired of watching. I know now, it's better to fall. What do you think, Isidro?"

Good God, I had no idea Ledesma had become an evangelist. I pat his shoulder, tell him to get some rest. He smiles to himself and looks around anxiously, like he's coming out of a trance.

This is the man who—according to Gabriela—is "my sort"?

WEDNESDAY, JANUARY 10TH

Brito came to class today with a black eye and split lip. He could barely speak when I asked him about it. Brito, as I've said, is strong, big-headed. I figure he's about to get kicked out for fighting. Tears leak from his injured eye and he grits his teeth, holding them back. I assumed he wouldn't tell me what happened in class, but he doesn't when I catch him alone, either. Stubborn, he buries his chin in his chest, refusing to meet my eye.

"It must have taken a few guys to do this. You're a bull, Brito."

His lip curls in pain and contempt. I give up.

In the dining hall, I bring it up with Martínez first, then with the assistant headmaster. Attacking his steak, Martínez shrugs, laughs, asks if I'm going to start getting involved in kid stuff. But the assistant headmaster shows obvious interest, the hint of a yellowed smile. He thinks it's wonderful that I'm so concerned about the students. Not every teacher commits himself so fully, he says.

"Yes, Brito's case is a sad one. He hurts himself to get attention. Afterward, he won't point the finger at anyone because deep down he's a good boy, he doesn't want to make trouble. He just wants to be noticed, fussed over. But there's no doubt, the nurse saw through it right away: he does it all to himself."

Surprisingly, Gabriela also believes this is true. She's known Brito since he was small. His mother died when he was seven. His father, one of the maintenance staff, is an ex-con, a recovering heroin addict, an incurable depressive who barely notices his son. Brito has no one. That's why he hurts himself.

I squeeze Gabriela against me. I want her to stop talking.

I still don't understand. I don't know a thing.

SUNDAY, JANUARY 14TH

The *colich*'s anniversary celebration. It had never been mentioned to me before. An absolute disaster: surprise and improvisation have led to this miserable state, a boiling brain and double vision.

From his portrait, Andrzej Wybrany—his lifeless expression, white whiskers, benevolent, slightly crossed eyes—presided over the ceremony. The assistant headmaster—dressed for the occasion in an alpaca suit—took the stage and spoke of circular justice, the significance of the scholarship students' presence, students he referred to as "special." Separated by sex and grade level, the students pretended they were hearing this for the first time. Señor J. showed obvious disinterest. When it was his turn to speak, he improvised a few overly grandiose remarks, encouraged school spirit, and introduced a hymn I didn't recognize, which the boys' chorus sang masterfully. Their clear voices reached the ceiling, swirling on high, a preciosity perfectly suited to the great auditorium.

It was hard not to be moved.

As we applauded, I noticed Ledesma wasn't there.

I assumed he'd slunk away from the celebration, from the obligation to clap. I also assumed his absence would not be well-received by the administration, unless he had a more than justifiable excuse.

Yesterday's staff memo had made it perfectly clear that attendance was mandatory. It even detailed what we should wear, where we should sit, and included some elevated words about the spirit of the event.

Ledesma had escaped all that. He'd been spouting nonsense the last time I saw him; maybe he wasn't aware of the seriousness of his actions. We'd soon see what the consequences were.

I myself couldn't get away, or wasn't brave enough to try. I listened to every speech, clapped as loudly as anyone. During the reception, however, I felt exposed and sought out a corner where I could drink my cocktails in peace.

The students were dancing together, boys and girls mixing at last. I noted the lustful gleam in their eyes, inappropriate for their age. Their fingers clenched, desirous of flesh, any flesh. Surrounded by his acolytes, Ignacio stared at Héctor. Their rivalry was a constant exchange of savage glances.

I stood watching them for several minutes. Then, I saw Señor J. signal to Ignacio from the corner of the room. Ignacio went to him quickly, not bothering to conceal his limp, and the two went out together into the garden. They returned a short time later, smiling more broadly, with almost an air of provocation. Ignacio looked like he was in an excellent mood. As he passed me, he patted my back with a familiarity I wasn't sure how to reproach.

Sacra crept my way.

"I see you're keeping your eye on everyone," she said. "But you haven't seemed to notice me."

She was dressed in coral chiffon and heavy makeup. She narrowed her eyes theatrically. She looked younger under the diffuse light, but the jowls and bags under her eyes betrayed her age.

"I didn't see you," I said.

"I know you're always out of it. I could help you with that. If you keep your head in the clouds, things could start to go badly for you. Very badly."

She placed her hand gently on my arm and began sliding it up and down, waiting for a response. I stepped aside. Again, she pressed in close. She was very drunk. She couldn't stop laughing and half-moons of sweat darkened her dress under the arms. Martínez joined us, chomping away with ridiculous gusto on who-knows-what.

"You've been avoiding us lately, Bedragare. What's going on?"

It was both irritating and grotesque: old Martínez's attempt to gobble up life's leftovers in the worst way possible. His shirt hung out of his pants and he waved his arms, haranguing me.

"You should spend more time with us—you should enjoy yourself as much as possible. You think too much. Why do you think so much? Life is too short! You have a lady friend, don't you? Marvelous! Well, bring your friend along to one of our get-togethers."

I fled his presence as soon as I could. I felt the *colich* walls closing in, narrowing the space around me.

I sat on a bench at a remove from the party. Marieta was dancing in the middle of the room. A delicate sway of her hips, not at all innocent. She watched me from the corner of her eye to check the effect she was having. She doesn't know—couldn't know—that her body is completely different to me now, so different from what I admired in the beginning: I saw the assistant headmaster's frog-like hands on her hips, hands that ran over her ass, crept up her back. It disgusted me to even think about. I gagged.

She waved. I raised my glass in response, drained it in a swallow. I calculated it must have been my ninth or tenth drink.

I remember going to the bathroom to throw up. There were traces of cocaine on the sink. I wiped it up with my finger and licked. A small amount, but the taste hit me—bitter, intense, unmistakable. Exploding on the tongue.

On the way back, I turned the corner and bumped into Señor J. He held me by the arms, shook me lightly as if trying to rouse me.

"I think you've had too much to drink, Bedragare."

He threw an arm around my shoulder and brought me back to

the auditorium. They had dimmed the lights. I barely distinguished the figures in the melding shadows. Señor J. sat me down in an armchair and called over a waiter. He ordered him to bring me something substantial to eat.

"You're sloshed," he said. "This will help, you'll see."

The assistant headmaster would never speak that way, I thought. *Sloshed*. I laughed. Señor J. laughed, too. I hadn't realized I'd spoken out loud.

"You've got him pegged."

But he rushed to advise me to make no mistake, the assistant headmaster wasn't really a bad guy. He had his weaknesses, surely, but who didn't?

"You have them, too, don't you?" he added.

In his wink and the obscene curve of his lip, I knew he referred to Gabriela. I exaggerated my intoxication to avoid answering. He was still laughing. He spoke of younger flesh, dismissed the importance of sex, exalted love for the uncorrupted. His words were confused, I was confused. Someone broke a glass. I felt the pieces shatter in my brain. Marieta was watching us.

"We all want the companionship of Gerasim, in the end," he said. "I don't think you're any different from the rest of us."

"Who's Gerasim?" I managed to mutter. The alcohol surged inside my skull.

"Everyone has their own Gerasim. You simply must look for him. Look wherever you can, without fear or judgment. And don't ruin anyone else's good time."

I tried to form a new question, but my tongue was thick, the taste of coke sticking to the roof of my mouth. Words skittered away from me. They dropped, unformed, from my lips, shedding disconnected, aborted sounds. I wanted to know, wanted to question him now, wanted so much. I was willing, but unable.

I wanted to say *García Medrano*. I wanted to say *Marcela*, but her name was an unintelligible rattle. It didn't matter: Señor J. had already stood up and left. I could hardly make out his back, his stride, but his answer was still dissolving in the air, thoroughly sensible advice that was like a sudden wound: *Know your place, Bedragare. Don't get clever.*

Clever? Clever? I'm not getting clever, I argued. I must have been shouting. It was Marieta, I believe, who whispered in my ear that I should go, and Tato who took me by the arm and led me to my room. I must have fallen into bed and slept for a few hours straight; unconscious, my head spinning, nauseous but not vomiting.

I had several nightmares. Each one was worse than the last. I lost my voice, my eyes dropped out of their sockets, a group of boys played soccer with a severed head, thousands of birds smashed against the classroom window. There was background music in those dreams, distant music from the party, still echoing inside my head.

Chill dampness has woken me. Wet sheets stick to my skin. I turn up the heat and take a hot shower. It doesn't help. I can't simply lie down and stare at the ceiling. When I do, I see García Medrano's body hanging, endlessly dripping piss.

I write and I wait, lethargic and still drunk. I hope Gabriela will come to comfort me soon.

MONDAY, JANUARY 15TH

Ledesma is missing. No one has the faintest idea where he could be. Initially, we thought he had simply gotten sick. I thought he was probably in his room, delirious with fever, like I had been. But Gabriela told me his room was empty.

"What do you mean, empty? Even his things are gone?"

"No, not his things—not that he had much." She hesitated. "But he isn't there."

The students couldn't hide their pleasure. They hate math, and likely hate Ledesma. More free time, fewer classes, that's what his disappearance means to them. The assistant headmaster put me in charge.

I tried to get out of it. "But I don't know math."

The assistant headmaster never loses his patience. He tries soothing me with a smile.

"You don't have to actually teach math. You just have to be present. Take advantage and review your own classes. Just be on duty."

I didn't bother to hide my displeasure. Duties, duties, plenty of duties, I thought to myself.

"The children mustn't discover that we don't know Ledesma's whereabouts," he added. "Just tell them that he had to leave the *colich* for personal reasons."

Personal reasons, very well, but Ledesma's car—a red sedan that had sat accumulating dirt since I arrived—is still parked in its spot.

I think of suicide. Logically. Ledesma seemed impacted by what happened to García Medrano. He was the first person to speak of him to me, and he was also the first to tell me about that girl from so many years ago . . . or maybe not so many, I don't really remember. I pose the question to Gabriela. Does she think Ledesma has killed himself?

She's brushing her teeth when I ask. I watch her finish brushing and spit slowly, taking her time while she thinks. I see her face and neck, her body protected by a bathrobe—she's modest, she never lets me see her completely naked. She turns and looks at me sadly.

"No, I don't think so. I hope not."

More wishful than certain, her words float in the air between us before they vanish. The situation with Ledesma is, after all, always between us. I have a strange premonition, but I'm not quite sure about what.

TUESDAY, JANUARY 16TH

I go on a walk with the mastiff. I check Ledesma's car for clues. I look inside: dusty, unkempt, the floor covered in bags and slips of paper, ash on the seats, a little stuffed donkey hanging from the rearview mirror.

A strange object for Ledesma's car, the stuffed donkey.

A token of love? A remembrance from childhood? I realize I know nothing about him. Does he have children? A partner? What interests him, what does he think about the world?

What did his last words to me mean? *The eyes of all of humanity are on the pit into which we're poised to fall.*

I hear footsteps behind me. Marieta. Calm eyes and the faint little smile I suddenly can't stand.

"This Ledesma has us all going mad," she says. "He's an endearing eccentric, but he makes trouble."

She's usually so put together, but I notice today she's not wearing lipstick, her shirt is wrinkled. Maybe, I think, she's just back from seeing her lover. I maintain an obstinate silence. She must sense my disinterest, my disgust.

My coldness surprises her: I see the change in her face, the trace of unease. Is she afraid of me? I prolong the silence, narrow my eyes.

She continues, a tremor in her voice:

"It isn't the first time he's done this, disappeared without a word. Ledesma is . . . like that. He has his moods, and he wants us to respect them."

No one has ever brought up Ledesma's tendency to disappear, but I don't let on, don't ask. I restrict myself to listening and exaggerate my aloofness.

"Eccentric personalities are often rather . . . interesting. There are so many examples, so many artists who were considered eccentrics. Creativity, genius. Intelligence, I don't know . . . I do believe that Ledesma is an eccentric, but what happens when an eccentric doesn't find his true calling? He suffers from interior struggles, can't produce, becomes . . . poorly adapted, socially inept. In love, in his friendships."

She pauses. The more she speaks, the more she stammers. I begin to feel the irrepressible urge to strangle her. She constantly shifts position, crossing and uncrossing her arms over her chest. The mastiff is tense, too. Obviously, something is afoot.

"I think that Ledesma . . . I think he wanted to start something with me. He was lonely, I think he always has been, because he's so odd . . . There's always something unsaid when he talks. Unsaid, unseen, like backstage in a theater . . . One never really knows what he's thinking . . . and I rejected his . . . I rejected him and he cut his arms. I was with him when he did it, I saw him . . . he grabbed a knife, a pocket knife, and he made cuts on his arms, on his hands . . . They were deep, he bled a lot. I, I told him to stop . . . I told him nothing in this world was worth hurting himself like that."

I observe her neck, her elegant, white neck wrapped in a silk scarf, her hair falling on either side, framing it. Her pupils are dilated. She's afraid of me and suddenly I feel powerful. I want this moment to last. She backs up, starts to make a sign that she's leaving. I wanted to hit her. Insult her, at least. But that isn't me. I'm not capable, not yet. My throat burns.

A scream rises from my guts, courses up the trunk of my body. My skin is on fire. I open my mouth. Close my eyes.

I howl.

An animal cry. I'm conscious of its animalness.

I keep howling.

I open my eyes part way. Marieta is running down the path, running ridiculously in her high heels. She slips in the mud, stumbles, but keeps on running. I don't move an inch from where I stand. I watch her get farther away. Saliva drips down my chin. I wipe it off. The mastiff watches me. The earth emits a hostile chill. I laugh, I want to laugh, keep laughing, laugh for hours, amplify my insanity.

Back in my room, I write. The phone will ring and they will summon me immediately. I will be dismissed.

Dismissal materializes before me. It's a liberation.

WEDNESDAY, JANUARY 17TH

I'm given a medical exam. An emergency psychiatrist comes from Cárdenas, just for me. An athletic young guy, redheaded. Too young, perhaps. He looks me over, takes my blood pressure, taps on my chest, examines my eye sockets, my ears. I don't resist. I feel extraordinarily relaxed. I could have fallen asleep right there on the table. And though I wouldn't be able to repeat the performance, I have no regrets about what happened yesterday.

He addresses me informally.

"You're not well. Your resistance is low. You need to take care of yourself."

He prescribes pills and two syrups. I ask what they are, what they're for. He answers vaguely.

"The issue is your stress. You take things too much to heart. Try to calm down. The medicine will help. It's nothing serious."

"Sometimes my eyesight fails," I say. "It's like I'm going crazy."

"What are your symptoms?" He changes his voice, conveying professionalism as he turns back to me.

"Blurry vision, blind spots, floaters . . . it's different every day."

He puts on gloves again and inspects me, seemingly without much interest. I follow his commands: look up, look down, this side, now that side, blink, don't blink. I have the suspicion that he's improvising.

He prescribes some eye drops and reaffirms his diagnosis. It's all due to stress and nothing, nothing at all, is of concern.

The assistant headmaster grants me leave to rest until next Monday. I wonder what he's told the students.

Ledesma still hasn't reappeared.

FRIDAY, JANUARY 19TH

I'm not sure what I was given, what's happening to me. I'm battered by relentless anxiety, rendered exhausted and confused. I will not take the medicine. I refuse to be sedated. I spend hours in bed and speak only when Gabriela comes to see me and bring food.

She's tidying my room and I watch her work. Light falls across her back at an angle, revealing particles that float around her as she sweeps. She's better than I am. I'm sunk. A few knocks from life and I'm a useless waste. But Gabriela never complains. Always a smile, always calm.

I lift myself up to see her better. She notices and turns, looks at me with a blush.

The sentence leaves my mouth with unexpected vehemence.

"We should have a baby."

She goes completely red. Continues sweeping without a word.

"I'm serious, Gabriela. You and I should have a baby. Get out of this place, the three of us."

She stops. Her hands tremble.

"That can't happen, sir—Isidro—it can't."

"But you're not that old," I argue.

She freezes. I regret the word *that*, which is like a knife. I rush to explain myself, but she stops me.

"I've been sterilized. I got sterilized when I came here."

It dawns on me that this is why she lets me come inside her. I feel a mix of jealousy, unease, surprise.

"But why? What for, Gabriela?"

"It was one of the conditions for working here. All the women who work here are sterilized. The school takes care of the procedure."

"What's their reason? To eliminate the risk that one of them will get you pregnant?"

She's embarrassed.

"I was okay with it. Why have more children? I wasn't going to have them, anyway. Valentina is enough work."

"How much work is Valentina? She's in the city. She has her life."

"No, you don't understand . . . it's the worry, the fear inside. I didn't want more of that. I agreed to the operation. I know some women who were forced to give their children up because they couldn't take care of them. I would prefer they not be born, before it came to that."

She brushes her fingers through my hair. She's comforting me, and that's when I realize that I'm crying.

She's known all along that I seek refuge in her, like a child and his mother, but I'm only conscious of it now, this instant. My desire had an unspoken, even instinctual, motive: future life. A desire, a path, that won't ever be fulfilled. Penetrating her no longer makes sense. Sex no longer makes sense. The promise of existence has been stripped from the act.

She sits down next to me and rests her head on my shoulder.

Outside, a little bird sings.

"A lark," she says.

She knows the names of the birds.

SUNDAY, JANUARY 21ST

The police came and searched the school this weekend. Martínez told me without me asking. The security cameras hadn't captured Ledesma leaving the *colich* in the days prior to his disappearance, and the mastiff hadn't shown any signs of an intruder. Nevertheless, the inspection of the *colich*'s facilities confirmed once and for all that Ledesma was not inside. One by one they searched the rooms, including mine. The classrooms, all sections of all buildings, even the pantries and broom closets. They combed the surrounding areas: the playing fields, the gardens. They trawled the swimming pools. All in vain. The working hypothesis was that Ledesma had slipped into the woods through a hole in the fence. They were looking for him out there. The police brought their German shepherds, alert and slobbering. The air hummed with walkie-talkies, beeps and whistles, a constant drone that we'd soon grow accustomed to.

The assistant headmaster informed us that they didn't need volunteers. I wouldn't have been inclined to join them, but I did approach one of the officers. I waited until he had time to speak to me, then showed him the fence hole that I knew about.

They carefully examined the site. According to the officer, recent fingerprints from various individuals had been found in the vicinity of the breach. Some of them could be Ledesma's, but to isolate them would be difficult.

He seemed neither interested nor knowledgeable.

When the sun went down, I watched them pack up from my room. Señor J. conversed with the officers and it took them a long time to leave. Hernández and Prieto were out there, too, and the mastiff raced around, upset by the presence of other dogs, the novelty. I saw a group of boys watching from a distance. Ignacio's gait, the Goon's mass. They won't be able to hide things from the students much longer.

Later, I called my sister. She must still be upset with me: she didn't pick up any of the times I tried her. I'm relieved and concerned in equal measure.

MONDAY, JANUARY 22ND

And yet, the students don't ask, they don't even ask what is going on. They received me in class as if everything were normal. Only a few alluded to the days I'd been out.

"Are you okay, now, sir?" Irene asks.

Yes, I'm okay now. I sit at my desk, press my elbows down and hold my head in my hands. I sit there, listless, for a few moments before I gather the strength to speak.

I assign a composition. They're surprised, after so much time.

"Didn't you say no more compositions?" they argue.

"It doesn't matter what I said," I respond. "I've changed my mind."

I don't even propose something clever. I tell them to write about their Christmas break. Where they were, what they did, who they were with.

"But sir, isn't that a bit nosy?" a girl asks.

I don't answer. I feel the need to shriek again, a muffled, distant desire that passes quickly. The girl's expression changes. She looks down, opens her pencil case, and begins to write.

They all begin to write.

I think about Ledesma. They introduced his substitute to me this morning: a nervous, skittish guy who attempted to win me over with stupid jokes. Maybe no one has told him about his predecessor, just like no one told me about García Medrano. No one will explain anything to him and he'll have to figure it out on his own. The search continues today—apathetic officers, fewer dogs than before, new equipment they're apparently using. The substitute will watch it all from afar, and it will be incomprehensible to him. He won't dare to ask, and nobody will have the compassion to tell him.

That's the way things are here.

The bell rings and I collect the compositions, stuffing them in my briefcase. I take them back to my room after lunch and rip them into tiny shreds. Then I lie down for a nap.

WEDNESDAY, JANUARY 24TH

I stopped by the faculty lounge today. It was completely empty. A chess match had been left half-finished; white was winning, a checkmate was imminent, even I could see it. There were glasses to be cleared away, messy fingerprints on the glass tabletop. I turned on the TV, sunk into the couch, and dozed off.

I spend too much time like that, dozing. The hours seem to pass quickly, but the truth is, I do almost nothing and time stands still. Total paralysis. I keep assigning compositions that I don't correct. I barely speak to the students. They're unmanageable now, and I allow it. I keep completely to myself. I eat alone and speak to no one. I always take an empty corner table, and I pretend to read so nobody bothers me. Martínez despairs over my apathy: he jokes and I don't smile, he goads me and I stare back, my lips pressed tight.

Only Gabriela is allowed to visit me, even though there's nothing sexual between us now. We just lie together on the frozen bed. We hold each other and stare at the ceiling in silence. Over and over, I trace the profile of her face. When her shift starts, she kisses me sweetly before she leaves.

Then I write, and as I write, I relive everything that has transpired. Sometimes I even forget that I'm writing. I feel like the exact same things keep happening: they parade through my mind and I simply register them, a mental video camera.

My writing takes on the same strange quality as my days.

I know all this will lead to being fired. I won't be surprised. It's just a matter of hours, maybe days, before my life will revert to what it was before. I'll forget about the *colich*, I'll forget everything. Maybe I'll get my name back.

Or maybe I won't. Maybe I'll never go back to being who I was, just as I can't reclaim the boy captured in my sister's photo album.

I believe in reincarnation, reincarnation in this very lifetime: different lives, lived in one.

I believe in displacement. In the disappearance of the person we were yesterday.

I believe in a lack of surprise when faced with who we'll become tomorrow, even though we're unsure what form that will take.

I believe in the dissolution of identity. I believe in rupture.

They've broken me. And I don't believe in being put back together.

I'm on the couch, envisaging this litany of ideas, cocooned by the words fizzing in my brain, when someone enters the room and sits down next to me. The cushions sink scarcely deeper; whoever it is doesn't weigh much. I sense his breath, his masculine smell. I know it's not Martínez. Who could it be? I don't open my eyes, I keep them shut, I want to believe that Ledesma is back, that Ledesma's ghost has returned to entrust me with a message of hope.

Slowly, I open them and turn to look.

It's the substitute. He gives an anxious smile and apologies. He hadn't intended to wake me, he says.

I must look strange. He hesitates, shifts in his seat.

"How's it going?" I ask.

"Not bad, not bad," he says.

His hair is gelled, a head of curls he attempts to tame by combing them back behind his ears. He looks ridiculous. I'm amused. His eyes dart, he's suspicious. Between these soulless walls, I am the enemy.

"Nice place, isn't it, the *colich*?" I say at last.

He scratches himself nervously. He doesn't know what to say. He assumes I expect a concrete response and doesn't want to disappoint me. Actually, I don't expect anything, not even an answer. I keep talking.

"It's quiet here. Not much noise, not much activity. The students are splendid children. Obedient, disciplined, they don't make them like that anymore. Sure, we're a bit isolated but who doesn't want to isolate themselves nowadays? Life in the city is too precarious."

He nods and whispers *that's true* or something to that effect, a few inaudible words. We hear the sound of the police dogs out in the woods. All of a sudden, they're barking like mad and I launch into speech, as if my brain had stalled and my words were advancing by themselves, rootless, stripped of thought. I listen to myself with interest . . .

"Do you hear those dogs? They must have found something. A piece of clothing, a footprint, blood on a branch. That tangled, wild forest, the river that feeds the dense vegetation. Right there beside us, so close to civilization. Kind of symbolic, don't you think?"

He wants to go. He's on his feet and he wants to leave, but doesn't know how. I see that he's frightened. I've lost him. I want to keep him here and I stretch out my arm. He shrinks away.

"Don't go just yet, stay a little longer. I'd like to talk with you. You must be lonely, having just arrived. Are you married?"

He stammers, one foot inching toward the door.

"No, not yet. My girlfriend and I are planning on it. When this job ends, we'll set a date."

I bite my lip so not to laugh, hard enough to almost hurt.

"Do you think you'll be subbing long? What did they tell you?"

"They didn't tell me anything, and I didn't want to ask."

He hesitates, then, and appears to think.

"Do you know him? Do you know why he's out?"

I look at the man and recognize myself, the person I was not long ago. I feel cold. The dogs, frantic, are still barking. I've begun to shake, something stabs my temples, I could have another attack.

I whisper:

"Get away."

He looks at me in surprise. I don't have to say it again. His reaction is swift and predictable.

"Okay. Okay, I'm going."

Get away. Get away, I repeat again and again, even after he's gone, ensconced in the couch, eyes closed. But the substitute hadn't understood. No, no he couldn't have. *Get away. Get away from here, from all of this.*

He will not hear me, he will not understand.

Solitude looms.

THURSDAY, JANUARY 25TH

Yesterday's barks meant exactly what—in my delirium—I had sensed.

Ledesma has reappeared.

Or rather, Ledesma's body. Ledesma himself is nowhere to be found in those massacred hunks of flesh.

The violence had been extreme, and it had been excessive. Much more than required to kill someone.

Ledesma hadn't been a big man: 160 centimeters, sixty kilos. A lightweight. You could have knocked him over with a single push. I imagine he didn't put up a fight, or instinctively defend himself.

But they had bashed his head with a rock until his skull caved in.

They had pulled out his fingernails and maimed his testicles. Ten meters from the cadaver, they found a piece of his leg. His intestines were fanned out around him in a two-meter radius. The stench, they said, was unbearable. The flies, deafening.

That's what was left of Ledesma.

Impossible not to think of Lux.

(. . .)

Hushed details spread through the *colich*. There is something pleasurable found in recounting the minutiae. No one dares to ask who could be guilty.

Gabriela is terrified. For the first time, I see her falter. An unprecedented, dreadful uncertainty lurks in her eyes. For the first time, I'm the one who offers comfort.

Señor J. gathers us all together right away. The chief of police is there in the auditorium, with the assistant headmaster. Marieta stands in the corner, impassive. Wybrany's portrait supervises the proceedings.

The chief announces there will be questioning. He assures us that all lines of inquiry are open and that the investigation is only just beginning. As he speaks, I'm invaded by a sense of unreality. I watch him up on stage, circumspect, professional. It's like watching an actor on screen. I look around me and see that we're all actors: leads, supporting characters, bit players. Film noir. Okay, I tell myself, we can pretend we're actors until the bitter end. I chuckle quietly. Martínez elbows me in the ribs, warning me to shut up. The assistant headmaster stares at me. I stare back.

Then Señor J. steps to the podium. He looks better than ever: rosy cheeks, trim goatee, eyes brimming with health. Solid, robust. He studies the audience before he begins, quite possibly to create atmosphere. His eyes slide across each one of us, landing on one or another by chance. Or not. The microphone picks up the sound of his exhale. He wants to make it clear there are no adequate words.

And yet, I could have easily predicted them.

He asks for discretion, prudence. He speaks of the *colich*'s prestige, of the damage a scandal would cause, of the need to keep the media away. He promises that whoever was responsible will be found, that—undoubtedly—it's someone from the outside. He urges maximum precaution when we go out; visits to the woods will remain strictly forbidden until further notice. He speaks of the dangers of the outside world, that in order to achieve the security we all seek, he foresees new sacrifices will need to be made.

That's when I start to laugh.

Softly, at first. Martínez's gesturing does nothing to calm me; in fact, it makes it worse.

I laugh harder. I'm about to crack. I can momentarily contain the roar by gritting my teeth, but I soon explode in conspicuous peals of laughter.

I stand up. Yelling, laughing at the same time. I lose it.

They all turn to stare. Martínez squeezes my arm, pulling me into my seat. I struggle to stay on foot, wobbling and obstinate. The chief of police is shocked. He rushes over, plants himself before me, legs spread in a wide stance. He orders me to shut up, to stop.

I don't stop. I laugh harder. I think someone slaps me, there's a faint taste of blood. That's all I remember. They must have pulled me out of the auditorium and injected me with something. I lie who-knows-where for hours. After dark, they bring me back to my room.

I'm just now awake, and I'm missing hours of memory. I squint my eyes, make an effort, but I can't bring them back. It is sad, it's true, but I can't write what I don't remember. I can't make it up. I wouldn't dare. All I know is that I have a terrible headache.

I write: *I have a terrible headache.*

I won't write what I don't know: I will leave a blank.

MONDAY, FEBRUARY 19TH

Early on, I wrote several pages a day, almost every day. The gaps between one day and the next were minimal: it was easy to maintain a particular tone, follow points of reference. But then things—some things—began to languish while others sped up. My entries became shorter, I started skipping a day now and then, the anchor lost its hold.

And then came the pause, the blank space.

I predicted it, unintentionally. I wrote *I will leave a blank*, thinking that I referred to several hours of what had been a manic night. Instead, it was the beginning of a blank that has lasted three weeks.

One writes from where one leaves off and it's as if no time had passed. One writes nonstop and creates the illusion of movement, natural rhythm, a series of background beats. One doesn't capture the interruptions, the syncopation.

But this is wrong.

One could symbolize the rupture—a blank page, an individual character (. . .), a semantic reference (*three weeks later*)—but it would be futile: the appearance of momentum would not change.

It all revolves around the same thing, in the end: the impossibility of reflecting time in what was left unwritten, what was omitted and will not remain. What we felt, and forgot.

The story of what happened can be written. The facts. A soulless, summary tale. A distortion, in the end.

But all words are distortions.

It would be good, for example, to be able to state here and now who it was who murdered Ledesma. We should know, after three weeks. We should at least be able to tie up those ends. But I don't know the answer, and even though it isn't hard to imagine, the identity will never be made public. Ledesma was about to do something, he'd told me himself: *But I'm tired of watching. I know now, it's better to fall.* And so it was. His dismembered body, converted to pure linguistics. A shredded message, ready for morphological, syntactical, semantic analysis. I see it clearly now, now that I know about such things.

It would also be good to write about what was occurring in the *colich* in the meantime, to describe the movements of Señor J., the assistant headmaster, those students who stood apart from the rest. It would be good to describe how Sacra and Martínez looked one another in the eye, interrogating each other. It would be good to describe Ledesma's substitute postponing his wedding. It would be good to follow the threads, delve into the story.

But I won't be able to, given that I removed myself before they could remove me. Goodbye, *colich*.

A predictable denouement, what one could have imagined. But that doesn't signify an inferior ending. I've never actually liked surprise endings. Life doesn't have surprise endings: everything is sketched from the beginning; it develops in the deep and when it rises to the surface, it's only because the end has come. Time ran out.

We are what we are writing about ourselves, though we don't know it.

I had to leave the *colich*. This is not a shock. It was established from the beginning of my story.

I was an imposter. I always had been.

Everyone knew it.

We all knew so much. And yet.

(. . .)

Gabriela and I took a walk. We disobeyed orders and went into the woods, with the dog. All the holes in the fence had been repaired. She had a key. We walked through the gate, out into the open.

We held hands. It was our farewell. We didn't speak.

We reached the place where—they said—Ledesma's butchered body had been found.

I patted the dirt, smelled the air. Nothing was left of him there, no sign, no trace. No floating ghost. Nothing. Nothing more than a piece of land like any other, fertile ground for the living forest which had also harbored death. The mastiff sniffed around, barked nervously. She saw what we could not sense.

A cold clamminess rose from the dirt and plumes of mist crowned the trees. The birds sang, like they always did. I still didn't know their names.

I kissed Gabriela on the forehead, held her hand against my cheek. We stayed like that a few moments. She already knew I was leaving. She understood, and she approved. First, García Medrano, then Ledesma: all signs now pointed to me. Nothing needed to be said.

The mastiff wound herself between our feet. We turned back before nightfall. The buildings accentuated the darkening sky. They seemed larger, less inhabited. The silence, enormous.

I didn't see Gabriela again.

(. . .)

And will it come as any surprise that I write now of my sister's disappearance? That, too, was foretold in these lines, almost from the beginning.

Her apartment had been ransacked. The living room wall smudged black, as if from fire. Scattered: torn mattress, empty fridge, pieces of broken china, rags, glass. They'd spent nights there. Even cooked. They must have had a child with them. There were crayon drawings on the wall of the sort children make: a house, a man, a woman, the sun, a moon, stars. From the simplicity of the pictures, the child was probably very young. He or she had drawn the sun shining and a house with a pitched roof, something never before seen in Cárdenas.

From the police station, I was redirected to an information office, then another office, then a department, until finally a thin girl with a stutter informed me that, according to the facts in her possession, the property had been non-violently invaded and the owner relocated to subsidized housing in the outskirts of the city.

"The owner can't return?"

The girl looked at me without the slightest hint of comprehension. There were several photos pinned on a corkboard next to her desk: images of dogs and cats, flowers, babies. That was her real world, it seemed. The office was, I expect, not reality. I had to repeat the question.

"I-i-if the property is s-s-s-still occupied, it's g-g-g-going to be hard for her to r-r-r-return," she said at last.

"The apartment is empty. I checked it myself."

"And yuh-yuh-you are . . . ?"

I told her again.

"The owner's brother."

Despite my best efforts and all the paperwork, I haven't been able to locate her. They gave me various phone numbers to call: the first is always busy, another is never answered, the third is a wrong number, the automated message is from an insurance agency. The fourth one puts me on hold while they check their lists for her name; I'm told she doesn't appear on any of them. They tell me to try again in a few days.

No one understands why she doesn't call me.

They insinuate that maybe she doesn't want to be found. They suggest I wait for her to call. They don't trust me.

I let them talk and don't contradict them. Finally, I admit they're right and give up.

I change the dead bolt on the door, buy a blow up mattress and a cook stove. I get used to the noise, or exhaustion does it for me. I sleep a lot. Sometimes, I dream of the noises at Wybrany. Sometimes, I even hear a lark outside my window. I haven't had any more nightmares.

FRIDAY, FEBRUARY 23RD

I started this without drama. Modestly, clumsily. I must end the same way: this diary became pointless a while ago. It was always the story of the *colich*, not the city. I didn't know it, but I was writing the story of the *not-city*, the flip side of the life I live now. What I had to tell, I have told. Poorly, because I could only ever grasp a part of it. Poorly, because I didn't completely understand that part I did see. Poorly, because I always was a *wannabe writer*—oh, darling Lola, how right you were.

Poorly, but this story has been told.

I have to go, I know.

There is an epilogue, of course. There is an epilogue to every story.

It was Gabriela's only request. I had to fulfill it.

(. . .)

She wasn't expecting me. She couldn't have been. I considered myself immune to everything, but I still felt a heaviness in the pit of my stomach when I decided to ring the doorbell. Aftershocks of anxiety spread through my body. I was almost drowning.

I could hear through the distortion of the call box that it was just a girl who answered. "Does Valentina live here?" I asked.

"Valen? Yeah, but she's not home."

I decided to wait for her near the front entrance.

I spent several hours watching the brick wall, chocolate-brown apartment blocks, chipped and peeling, haphazardly hung laundry, bird shit accumulating on windowsills. The noise, people, smells: a uniform, monotonous show. It was hypnotizing, to watch without having to be aware of my every move.

A tall girl in sports clothes arrived at the building, pulling a shopping cart behind her. Valen? I shouted. She turned to look. It wasn't her.

And then another girl came. Squat and enormous, with very short hair and ruddy skin, chomping on gum as she dug for the key in her bag. She didn't hear me call to her. I got up and went over, said her name. She looked at me without a reaction: dull eyes in deep black circles, a double chin. She asked what I wanted. I told her. She considered this for a few seconds and then let me inside.

The apartment was dark and damp. There was hardly anywhere to sit; the couch was covered in laundry waiting to be folded, piles of boxes were heaped on the chairs. An adolescent, her face covered in pimples, sat in a rocking chair watching television. Valen brought me a plastic folding chair and sat herself down on a stool, studying me with the same indolence. With unbroken focus, the girl kept watching TV. She didn't seem to have noticed me.

"She's one of my roommate's sisters," Valen explained. "She comes over some afternoons."

Though I hadn't asked, she started to tell me in a flat voice that there were four of them, they all worked in this place or that, living together wasn't always easy.

"Sometimes they bring their boyfriends home. There's not enough space as it is and then they bring their boyfriends. You've got to be fucking kidding me. I have to sleep on the couch because they have company."

Valen obviously didn't have a boyfriend. Observing her, I realized she was going to have a very rough time. I tried to discern something of Gabriela in her. Gabriela wasn't beautiful, but there was sweetness in her drooping lids and the corners of her mouth, always ready to smile or apologize. Valen had none of that. Puffy, yellow, sordid suffering and profound indifference reflected on her face. Rolls of fat cascaded down her belly; she was so large that she had to spread her thighs in order to sit. She breathed heavily. Bitterness and despondency lurked in her eyes. I suddenly felt something akin to compassion, but I was repulsed, as well. I tried to smile. Judging from her glacial expression, it came across as more of a grimace.

The *colich* did this to her, I thought.

She knew that I was an emissary of her mother. She gave me her report and waited for my questions.

But I didn't know what to ask. I wasn't interested in her current life—it was all right there around me—but rather in her time at the school. It was hard to believe she had ever attended class in the clean, modern lecture hall, or played on the paddle courts or sung the hymn during the Wybrany anniversary festivities. That mass of flesh, devoid of all passion and charm, was my only connection to that completely unreal world, fruit of some nightmare.

I stammered, not knowing where to begin.

She stood up. She hadn't eaten lunch yet and was hungry. Did I want something? I shook my head and she went into the kitchen.

Now that we were alone, the girl watching the soap opera turned to me, suddenly aware that I was there. With a smirk, she winked at me. I looked away. She taunted me, running her tongue over her lips.

I heard the ding of the microwave and Valen returned with a steaming bowl of lasagna. The other girl sunk back into silence. The glow of the screen lit up her face, her skin devastated by acne.

Valen stuffed herself, scattering grated cheese with every bite. And as she stuffed herself, she watched me with a static expression and waited for me to break the silence.

I tapped my fingers on my knees, took another look around the room, and inhaled, ready to begin.

"You knew Celia, didn't you Valen?"

She chewed before answering. I'd seen a flash in her eyes, a spark of anger, perhaps. She hadn't expected the question. She was surprised and obviously trying to compose herself. Resentment brought her back to the present.

"Yeah, of course I knew her. We shared a room. She was just another girl, but everybody looked out for her. I'm not surprised that you've heard of her."

"And what happened?"

"What happened? They expelled her. She got kicked out. She was always in trouble. She never studied. She interrupted in class. Really mouthy, really rude. She did whatever she wanted. Her mother and father didn't work there, which was weird. Nobody had any idea how she ended up at the *colich*. But there she was, and she didn't answer to anyone. Out of control. I guess nobody really took responsibility for her."

She got up for some chocolate. She kept eating and talking, unexpectedly animated.

"She planned an escape, once. She roped a few of us in, convinced us we should go with her. She said it would only be a few days outside the school, that we had to see the world. She planned to make it all the way here to Cárdenas, but she didn't know how. We left before sunup through a hole in the fence and made it through the woods, totally freezing. It was pointless. They caught us right away."

"Were you punished?"

"No. We were never punished in the *colich*. They only lectured us, changed the rules if we did something wrong. Whatever had been allowed up till then suddenly wasn't anymore; that was their tactic. It was almost worse. I would have preferred to be punished."

She peeled the foil on another chocolate and watched me for a few seconds before speaking. She searched my eyes: something had dawned on her.

"I bet my mother told you that Celia was involved with the Advisor."

"Your mother didn't tell me anything."

Valen laughed with disdain.

"I don't believe you. You asked about Celia so that I would tell you. You know something."

"Well, it wasn't your mother. I was told by a colleague."

"And you want me to give you details?"

Her lips were stained with chocolate. She smiled in disgust.

"No, I don't want the details," I lied.

She sighed and raised her eyebrows.

"Good, because if you want them, I can't give them to you. I got along with her okay. There were other girls who ruined me, always insulting me. Other girls like me, scholarship girls. I didn't expect any better from them, actually. But Celia was different. She pretty much kept out of that shit. I think she might have liked me a little. But she didn't confide in me about her life. She kept to herself. She only told her secrets to this half-wit, one of the posh girls—Teeny. Small, skinny, always sniffling. *She* knew everything. Not me. I don't have anything to tell you."

She stood up quickly, wiping her mouth with the back of her hand. She apparently considered our conversation over. I was disappointed. That's all she could tell me? Had they really covered up the scandal so successfully? Had everyone actually been fooled?

Valen had no desire to hear any more from me, but I wasn't willing to hide the truth. She watched me, her flat eyes ringed with dark circles.

None of this was what I expected. I spoke out of desperation:

"Celia wasn't expelled, Valen. Celia killed herself."

The other girl shifted to see us better, turning her eyes toward what—for her—was just another soap opera. Valen looked stunned. Like she had aged years in an instant. The room was completely quiet, except for the sound from the TV, a conversation outside any frame of reference. Valen threw up her arms—thick, white—and shook her head furiously, shouting.

"Why are you telling me this shit? What am I supposed to do?"

"Nothing, I don't want you to do anything," I whispered. "I only wanted you to know the truth."

"The truth? What truth? What the fuck are you talking about? What do you know about the truth? You think you're the one who knows the truth? You fucked my mother and that gives you the right to come here and tell me the truth? Did you stop to think about *my truth?*"

Sounds started to come from behind the other doors, footsteps making their way down the hall. Valen's roommates smelled blood, and they swarmed like flies. I stood up, grabbing my jacket. I went for the door.

Valen was distraught. She couldn't stop screaming. She grabbed my arm, tried to force me to listen. I saw that her eyes were wet. Her chin trembled in fury.

"Why didn't you do something?"

"There was nothing I could do, Valen. I arrived a long time after," I argued.

"After *what*?" she wailed. "I'm not talking about Celia! I'm talking about everything! Everything else! Why didn't you do something to stop it? Why did you come here to tell me truths? Why don't you tell other people the truth? Why doesn't anyone dare to do that? Why don't you leave me alone? You, my mother . . ." She spun around toward her roommates, who glanced at each other, amused. "All of you!"

I knew there was nothing I could do to calm her. I shook her off, made it to the entryway, and put my hand on the doorknob. I turned to look at her one last time, waiting for a goodbye, or an apology.

And then, it struck me. The final chord. A thick loogie, flecked with bits of food, slid down my face. Hatred, unadulterated rancor, resentment, bitterness—all of it, and all of it hers. The soap opera ended, and the theme music swirled between us.

That gob of spit. It was the *colich* and Cárdenas; the acne-ridden girl and her wink, Ledesma's desecrated body, Gabriela's stoicism; it was Marcela, spirited away in secret, pulled by the hand; it was Sacra's lewdness and Martínez's cynicism; it was García Medrano's papers, no longer a mystery to me.

No, the gob of spit wasn't a humiliation. It made absolute sense: the inescapable, final message. To be heard, and obeyed.

Valen was trembling, sobbing, beside herself.

I took a handkerchief from my pocket and wiped my cheek.

I hung my head, and left.

HEROES AND MERCENARIES
(GARCÍA MEDRANO'S PAPERS)

FOUR BY FOUR. Her little world. The girl paces the room, goes to bed, gets up. Waits.

Sometimes they open the door. It's usually to leave her food, good food served on plastic plates with small plastic utensils. But sometimes they open the door to let her out for a bit, too.

She likes when they let her out. She gets some fresh air. Has contact. It's more than four meters by four meters, the outside world.

Outside, they treat her well. They cherish her.

She likes when they let her out.

Her body is damp. Damp with sweat and desire to be let out.

THE CITY IS FORTIFIED. It's surrounded by a wall three meters high. The wall is made of stone. There's some graffiti, not much.

Graffiti written in an unknown language. No one knows what it says. But even if they could understand the words, the city's inhabitants wouldn't be able to read them: the graffiti appears only on the outside. There's not a single word on the inside of the wall. No drawn hearts, not a single *I was here*, not even a little obscene drawing. Nothing.

Politics don't exist in the city. Or at least the inhabitants aren't aware of the existence of politics.

The existence of something comes into being only through the awareness that it exists. That's why.

THE WALL WAS BUILT just a few years ago by thousands of men. But all the city's inhabitants believe it's been there for centuries, despite the fact that they are only just seeing it now.

Sometimes they gathered to watch the men lifting and setting the stones, but they've forgotten this too.

The building of the wall and the building of a consciousness of its antiquity were simultaneous. That's why.

FOUR BY FOUR. The girl doesn't know that she has another little four-by-four world beside her, containing a different girl who doesn't know that she exists, either.

If she knew, she would try to communicate with her.

If the other girl knew, she would try as well.

Perhaps they would invent a code of long and short knocks on the wall. A new Morse code, since they don't know about the old one. It would make them feel better. They would be capable of imagining that perhaps there were even more girls; that perhaps there were more four-by-four cells, built one after another in an orderly fashion, to infinity.

But both think they're alone and so they keep silent, and anxiously wait.

MORE SPACE IS AVAILABLE, of course, but it's the confinement to four by four that produces pleasure for the one who locks and unlocks the door.

The pleasure isn't the girl. The pleasure is in controlling the girl's availability. The pleasure is in erasing the girl's notion of a world beyond the dimension of four by four, in erasing the notion of something other than those brief moments when he's with her and her world expands.

The pleasure is in having various girls who think they're the only one.

The pleasure is in making these girls happy with what would make other girls unhappy.

Changing the rules, the way the world works.

THE CITY'S INHABITANTS are constantly trading. Transaction is their way of life. There is no production of any kind. They trade with things they can touch and with things that are intangible, with things that are clean and things that are dirty, with people, objects, concepts.

The inhabitants like to trade. They're happy trading. They cannot conceive of another way of life.

Everything is vulnerable to being traded, including the inhabitants themselves.

The value of the transaction is stipulated by agreements drawn down to the last detail; there is no place for improvisation. Agreements are never considered in terms of fairness or unfairness, but in terms of plausibility. An agreement is made when it's plausible.

If two or more people believe in something, it's plausible, and therefore it's susceptible to becoming an agreement, a transaction, a trade.

THEY WERE TOLD IT WAS WORTH trying this way of life. A simple and easy life. They accepted. They forgot the old one.

Once in a while a girl disappears. Or a boy.

This became frequent and it became normal. And in becoming normal, it was accepted as the natural order of things. No one was overly sorry about it, just like no one is overly sorry about the fact that occasionally it rains or hails, given that naturally, it has to rain and hail.

THE CONTRAST BETWEEN THEIR SKIN is gratifying. Between bodies and ages. The contrast is sometimes grotesque, but always stimulating.

There are those who take pleasure in seeing it like this. The girl is thin, compliant; the man is slack, covered in veins. A difference of forty years, perhaps more.

Symbols of power: pants down and bunched over his shoes, cigar in hand, an early sign of victory as he assails her over and over.

The girl doesn't remember anything else and she prefers it to solitude.

She holds him when he's finished, calls him *papi*. The one watching moves away, leaving them alone.

He doesn't believe anyone should question this coupling, since it's perfectly clear that it works.

One doesn't interfere with the laws of the market.

THERE IS A SINK, a toilet. The girl turns on the faucet and watches as one drop of water drips slowly, then another, and another. Droplets, marking time.

She looks closer. At first, it's nothing but a shiny quiver in the mouth of the spout, but it grows fuller and fatter, heavier, drops, and explodes.

One droplet. Then another.

Robinet, the girl whispers. She remembers that word from school.

She doesn't remember "sink" or "toilet." She doesn't remember the school. She only remembers *robinet, robinet.*

WORDS become isolated. They don't know that other words exist. They grow bigger this way, more powerful perhaps.

They lost the middle beat between *yes* and *no*. And thanks to this, *yes* grew; it became enormous. The same thing happened to *no*. Now they are two towers. Two tall, identical towers, at odds.

The city's inhabitants manage their words carefully. Their language is rudimentary, but effective.

Deprived of nuance, everyone wins. Less misunderstanding, fewer misgivings.

All of that has been forgotten, even by the old ones.

THE METAPHYSICAL PARADOX of indisposability loops around itself, resulting in a de facto impossibility. The city's inhabitants can dispose of things, they can even dispose of their own bodies, given that it's always possible to kill themselves.

And yet, the body itself is something that can't be disposed of, in the absolute sense of the word, unless it is left in such a state that there is no longer any possibility of its disposal: in this case, its use.

Therefore, this absolute disposal of the body actually comes down to putting it *out of use*. So the city's inhabitants can commit suicide, but they cannot, strictly speaking, dispose of themselves.

ROBINET, ROBINET, the girl whispers.

This constant refrain returns her to an amorphous past that no longer exists.

The girl is growing up and doesn't know what her future will be. She doesn't understand the notion of future.

Several months ago she bled for the first time. No one explained to her why. It helps her measure the passage of time.

She is being stripped of her words. She grunts, moans, becomes a beautiful, menstruating animal.

She knows how to say *robinet* with a guttural "r." That is all.

BUT YOU, SIR, you believe that you could do without your body? That's the part I don't understand.

What I believe, what I believe, I answer thoughtfully, is that I can't do without my body, but I can do without the inability to do without it. Do you see the nuance?

Nuance? Nuance, you say? What nuance? We've said language lacks nuance.

It lacks nuance? But, why? Why?

It's much easier for us to understand each other this way.

I see. We're getting to the root of meaning.

Not exactly. We're not getting anywhere. There is no meaning. We're trimming the edges. Serious pruning.

IN THE BEGINNING, armed men oversaw the men who were building the wall, and they oversaw its insurmountability. Any threat they shot on the spot. There were deaths, many deaths. Some were justified and others were not.

There are no watchmen. The wall wasn't built to prevent people from crossing; it isn't high enough to stop someone from jumping over. The wall only prevents one from seeing. Its opacity is its only purpose: there is no other. It creates a giant, compliant, orderly four by four.

No inhabitant would argue that this wasn't for the best. It isn't that the threat was kept out. It's even more effective: the threat dissolved and no longer exists.

And yes, even the oldest inhabitants have forgotten.

"The feeling of satisfaction—a kind of sensuousness—produced by having survived can become a dangerous, insatiable passion. It grows stronger every time. The higher the mountain of dead from which a survivor rises, alive, the more intense and tyrannical the need for that experience. The lives of heroes and mercenaries reveal a sort of addiction to it."

HEROES AND MERCENARIES command the most respect among the city's inhabitants. The heroes are made up; one believes in them as one believes in the gods. By contrast, the mercenaries are contemptuously real: they are many and they are well regarded. They comprise society's upper echelon.

Several times a year celebrations are held in their honor. The mercenaries form a procession, bringing offerings to the heroes. The city's inhabitants become devoted spectators. They feel an intense, internal satisfaction that is only explained in terms of survival. They feel chosen because they live in the city.

IT IS POSSIBLE that sometimes a girl, or boy, dies. The girl doesn't know this, because—as we've said—she doesn't know that there are other children. But that's the way it is: in the quest for gratification, there are games or practices that lead to death.

The girl isn't any more fortunate than the children who die. The girl simply lives, she grows, she develops breasts, hips.

The difference cannot be understood in terms of fortune. Dying is not worse than living. It's simply a different experience.

Things happen and they are observed, not judged.

And it isn't just the girl: nobody considers an alternate viewpoint. No one imagines anything different from what is. Things are what they are, and they happen because they happen.

And they're more content this way.

THE GIRL, TOO. Yes, she's content in the basic, ordinary way caged animals are content.

Full contentment, no room for doubt.

The girl is animalized. She has forgotten all words except *robinet* and *papi*.

She keeps track of time with the drops of water, the blood that runs down her thighs, the times she's let out to give herself to *papi* and the mercenary who watches as she does.

And yet, her nails are soft from lack of sunlight.

NO ONE EVER CONTEMPLATES the possibility of suicide. To think about suicide is to think about a radically different possibility of existence. This is unthinkable in the city, in the same way that it is unthinkable to imagine a world on the other side of the long three-meter-high stone wall.

A strange tale tells the story of a door in a wall, a door that leads to a differently textured reality. Not a paradise, but another reality, unimaginable and superior.

No one in the city has read this story. No one discovers that in certain dream states with a simple wish the door will materialize.

No one in the city knows that by renouncing control of their body, they create a new door through which they can pass through the wall.

Not even the oldest inhabitants know this.

THE CUSTOMS OF A PEOPLE can't be judged from the outside.

We are deeply affected by the cruel ways this city manages its sewers, but we also know that its inhabitants are happier this way.

This includes the boys and girls confined to their four meters by four meters underground.

To make them see things another way—to reinstate nuance, the difference between various words or the use of synonyms—would only contribute to the people's discomfort and unhappiness.

That sense of strangeness, of otherness, would be painful.

Not even the mercenaries know this. They needn't impose their power in any way. They are mercenaries because they were designated as such by mutual agreement.

No one questions this agreement, given that it's a plausible one they all can believe in.

THERE IS A HIGH WINDOW in one of the walls that forms the perimeter of the four by four. Sometimes a shaft of light filters in.

Not enough light to strengthen the girl's nails, but the sun rises and sets each day nonetheless.

When night has fallen, the cry of a bird also slips through the window. A screech owl, but the girl has practically forgotten about birds and she has certainly never heard the words *screech owl* in her life.

A screech owl's cry has a particular meaning: warning invaders that this is not their domain. Marking territory. A trilling whinny—*hoo-hoo-hoo-hoo*—sometimes answered by a sharp *tu-whu*.

But no one in the city is aware of this meaning, or the meaning of the response. It is—to their ear—a completely inarticulate exchange.

If no one knows, therefore, the meanings themselves have no importance and cease to be.

In fact, the screech owl's cry ceases to be the call of a bird at all. It becomes a sound without semantics, of doubtful origin. One doesn't think about it; one hears it, but doesn't listen. It's forgotten before it even comes into being.

And yet, this creature's neck allows it to turn its head around completely, to better observe its observer.

SOMETIMES, IT ALSO HAPPENS that the man tires of a girl or a boy and takes a shine to a new one.

It happens sometimes, but the girl doesn't know this.

It's going to happen to her—and soon—whether she knows it or not.

In such a case, a new transaction with agreeable terms is accepted by the parties.

In the event that a new transaction is not established, they allow the girl or boy in question to die.

Sometimes it happens. No one in the city knows this and therefore no one calls it into question. They can't.

THIS IS THE NEGATION OF BEING, I contend; the same process that nullifies the screech owl's cry.

ONCE, THE MAN GAVE THE GIRL a plant in a flowerpot. In those days, the girl was still young and unused. She was in her four-by-four incubator, being prepared for a promising future she naturally couldn't grasp at the time.

Through gestures the man explained that she had to water the plant to keep it alive. The man didn't use words with the girl. He wanted her to forget the ones she knew so that the process of forgetting would be less traumatic.

The man loved the girl: the proof was in the plant. The girl felt this and she did everything she could to take care of it.

But the plant died, nevertheless. Not right away, not one day to the next. It was a long process. The girl observed, unfazed, as one by one the branches grew dry and brittle. She didn't feel sorrow or pain. She recognized reality without even trying to understand.

The girl didn't know it, but she confronted her loss with the same cold acceptance that her parents had confronted theirs the day a mercenary selected her to live her life in a four-by-four cell.

CERTAIN REBELLIONS are impossible to start if one doesn't know what lies behind the wall.

The past is erased (not even the oldest of the city's inhabitants remember now); to rebel is no longer possible, except by negating existence.

Here, no one recognizes that idea. Therein, its power.

UN SILENCE PARFAIT règne dans cette histoire / Sur les bras du jeune homme et sur ses pieds d'ivoire / La naïade aux yeux verts pleurait en le quittant. / On entendait à peine au fond de la baignoire / Glisser l'eau fugitive, et d'instant en instant / Les robinets d'airain chanter en s'égouttant . . .

Of the poem, only the word *robinet* remains.

The rest is already dead.

There is no naiad, bathtub, or fugitive water; there is no love or longing.

The poem is hollow: a succession of sounds without meaning, just as the ululation of the screech owl is nothing more than a lost cry.

In this story, a perfect silence now reigns . . .

REFERENCES

During the long process of writing a book, certain external stimuli come to reside in a work, without having been consciously sought. We become magnets, sponges when we write; we attract and absorb stimuli; we centrifugate material in a manner that might be disorganized, perhaps, but never coincidental. Sometimes, these influences are so diluted that it's impossible to trace them, or they might belong to a personal realm difficult to transmit to someone else—images, memories, feelings. But there are others that are more obvious, and these notes are my attempt to acknowledge this second category:

The book the Headmaster—Señor J.—refers to when recounting the story of the servant Gerasim is, of course, Tolstoy's wonderful *The Death of Ivan Ilyich*, one of the best fables about the meaning of life, and death, that I've ever read.

The disturbing novel Isidro Bedragare reads out on the bench is *The Lime Works* by Thomas Bernhard.

Part of Ledesma's final words to Bedragare are inspired in the scene of the "madman" Domenico's speech in the Tarkovsky film *Nostalghia*.

The paradox of the indisposability of one's own body in relation to suicide that appears in García Medrano's papers comes from Gabriel Marcel's *Metaphysical Journal*.

And also found in García Medrano's papers, the quote about heroes and mercenaries is from *Crowds and Power*, by Elias Canetti, and the allusion to the fantastic tale refers to *The Door in the Wall* by H. G. Wells.

Lastly, the poem at the end of the novel is by Alfred de Musset, chosen for both its lightness and extraordinary capacity to serve as counterpoint to the story told in this book.

Seville, 2012

SARA MESA is the author of eleven works, including the novels *Scar* (winner of the Ojo Critico Prize), *Four by Four* (a finalist for the Herralde Prize), *An Invisible Fire* (winner of the Premio Málaga de Novela), *Un Amor*, and *Cara de Pan* (forthcoming from Open Letter). Her works have been translated into more than ten different languages, and she has been widely praised for her concise, sharp writing style.

KATIE WHITTEMORE is a graduate of the University of New Hampshire (BA), Cambridge University (M.Phil), and Middlebury College (MA), and was a 2018 Bread Loaf Translators Conference participant. In addition to her translations of Sara Mesa's work, she has forthcoming translations by Aroa Moreno Durán, Nuria Labari, Javier Serena, Aliocha Coll, and Jon Bilbao.

The publication of Sara Mesa's *Four by Four* in Katie Whittemore's translation was made possible thanks to a generous contribution by Dr. John and Kit Manhold. This contribution allowed for Open Letter to better fulfill its mission of introducing English readers to vital, important works of literature from around the world.

A true renaissance man, Dr. John Manhold was born and educated in Rochester, New York. His serendipitous life began with further education at Harvard Dental, followed by service in WWII and Korea, then additional study in pathology and psychology. His extensive research propelled him to give lectures and consultations around the world. These visits, plus the couple's love of travel, encouraged John to become certified in navigation (USCG) while his wife Kit studied marine engineering. They made a very notable journey, the "Big Wheel," a 6,000-mile loop north from Florida, through the Great Lakes, down the Mississippi, the Gulf, and back to Florida. Both are medaled sports enthusiasts, and John has won numerous awards for his sculptures that reside in public as well as private collections in the U.S. and abroad. More information about his life, his awards, his texts, and his novels can be found on his website: johnhmanhold.com.

Inga Ābele (Latvia)
High Tide
Naja Marie Aidt (Denmark)
Rock, Paper, Scissors
Esther Allen et al. (ed.) (World)
The Man Between: Michael Henry Heim & a Life in Translation
Bae Suah (South Korea)
A Greater Music
North Station
Zsófia Bán (Hungarian)
Night School
Svetislav Basara (Serbia)
The Cyclist Conspiracy
Michal Ben-Naftali (Israel)
The Teacher
Guðbergur Bergsson (Iceland)
Tómas Jónsson, Bestseller
Jean-Marie Blas de Roblès (World)
Island of Point Nemo
Per Aage Brandt (Denmark)
If I Were a Suicide Bomber
Can Xue (China)
Frontier
Vertical Motion
Lúcio Cardoso (Brazil)
Chronicle of the Murdered House
Sergio Chejfec (Argentina)
The Dark
The Incompletes
My Two Worlds
The Planets
Eduardo Chirinos (Peru)
The Smoke of Distant Fires
Marguerite Duras (France)
Abahn Sabana David
L'Amour
The Sailor from Gibraltar
Mathias Énard (France)
Street of Thieves
Zone
Macedonio Fernández (Argentina)
The Museum of Eterna's Novel
Rubem Fonseca (Brazil)
The Taker & Other Stories
Rodrigo Fresán (Argentina)
The Bottom of the Sky
The Dreamed Part
The Invented Part
Juan Gelman (Argentina)
Dark Times Filled with Light
Oliverio Girondo (Argentina)
Decals
Georgi Gospodinov (Bulgaria)
The Physics of Sorrow
Arnon Grunberg (Netherlands)
Tirza
Hubert Haddad (France)
Rochester Knockings: A Novel of the Fox Sisters
Gail Hareven (Israel)
Lies, First Person
Angel Igov (Bulgaria)
A Short Tale of Shame
Ilya Ilf & Evgeny Petrov (Russia)
The Golden Calf
Zachary Karabashliev (Bulgaria)
18% Gray
Ha Seong-nan (South Korea)
Flowers of Mold
Hristo Karastoyanov (Bulgaria)
The Same Night Awaits Us All
Jan Kjærstad (Norway)
The Conqueror
The Discoverer
Josefine Klougart (Denmark)
One of Us Is Sleeping
Carlos Labbé (Chile)
Loquela
Navidad & Matanza
Spiritual Choreographies
Jakov Lind (Austria)
Ergo
Landscape in Concrete
Andreas Maier (Germany)
Klausen
Lucio Mariani (Italy)
Traces of Time
Sara Mesa (Spain)
Four by Four
Amanda Michalopoulou (Greece)
Why I Killed My Best Friend
Valerie Miles (World)
A Thousand Forests in One Acorn: An Anthology of Spanish-Language Fiction
Iben Mondrup (Denmark)
Justine
Quim Monzó (Catalonia)
Gasoline
Guadalajara
A Thousand Morons
Why, Why, Why?

Elsa Morante (Italy)
Aracoeli
Giulio Mozzi (Italy)
This Is the Garden
Andrés Neuman (Spain)
The Things We Don't Do
Jóanes Nielsen (Faroe Islands)
The Brahmadells
Madame Nielsen (Denmark)
The Endless Summer
Henrik Nordbrandt (Denmark)
When We Leave Each Other
Asta Olivia Nordenhof (Denmark)
The Easiness and the Loneliness
Wojciech Nowicki (Poland)
Salki
Bragi Ólafsson (Iceland)
The Ambassador
Narrator
The Pets
Kristín Ómarsdóttir (Iceland)
Children in Reindeer Woods
Sigrún Pálsdóttir (Iceland)
History. A Mess.
Diego Trelles Paz (ed.) (World)
The Future Is Not Ours
Ilja Leonard Pfeijffer (Netherlands)
Rupert: A Confession
Jerzy Pilch (Poland)
The Mighty Angel
My First Suicide
A Thousand Peaceful Cities
Rein Raud (Estonia)
The Brother
João Reis (Portugal)
The Translator's Bride
Rainer Maria Rilke (World)
Sonnets to Orpheus
Mónica Ramón Ríos (Chile)
Cars on Fire
Mercè Rodoreda (Catalonia)
Camellia Street
Death in Spring
Garden by the Sea
The Selected Stories of Mercè Rodoreda
War, So Much War
Milen Ruskov (Bulgaria)
Thrown into Nature
Guillermo Saccomanno (Argentina)
77
Gesell Dome
Juan José Saer (Argentina)
The Clouds
La Grande
The One Before
Scars
The Sixty-Five Years of Washington
Olga Sedakova (Russia)
In Praise of Poetry
Mikhail Shishkin (Russia)
Maidenhair
Sölvi Björn Sigurðsson (Iceland)
The Last Days of My Mother
Maria José Silveira (Brazil)
Her Mother's Mother's Mother and Her Daughters
Andrzej Sosnowski (Poland)
Lodgings
Albena Stambolova (Bulgaria)
Everything Happens as It Does
Benjamin Stein (Germany)
The Canvas
Georgi Tenev (Bulgaria)
Party Headquarters
Dubravka Ugresic (Europe)
American Fictionary
Europe in Sepia
Fox
Karaoke Culture
Nobody's Home
Ludvík Vaculík (Czech Republic)
The Guinea Pigs
Jorge Volpi (Mexico)
Season of Ash
Antoine Volodine (France)
Bardo or Not Bardo
Post-Exoticism in Ten Lessons, Lesson Eleven
Radiant Terminus
Eliot Weinberger (ed.) (World)
Elsewhere
Ingrid Winterbach (South Africa)
The Book of Happenstance
The Elusive Moth
To Hell with Cronjé
Ror Wolf (Germany)
Two or Three Years Later
Words Without Borders (ed.) (World)
The Wall in My Head
Xiao Hong (China)
Ma Bo'le's Second Life
Alejandro Zambra (Chile)
The Private Lives of Trees